THE
AUTUMN
PEOPLE

THE
AUTUMN
PEOPLE

Ruth M. Arthur

ILLUSTRATED BY MARGERY GILL

LONDON
VICTOR GOLLANCZ LTD
1973

ISBN 0 575 01599 3

Printed in Great Britain by
Lowe & Brydone (Printers) Ltd., Thetford, Norfolk

For Dorothy and Robin
with love.

Contents

Entry   1

Part One   YESTERDAY: MILLIE   17

Part Two   TOMORROW: ROMILLY   81

Exit   161

ENTRY

FOR YEARS AND YEARS GRAN HAD BEEN PROMISING TO TAKE me to Karasay. Ever since I was quite small it had been my fairyland, an island of dreams, a place of mystery and magic. But for one reason or another I was fifteen before I succeeded in getting there. I found it all that I had hoped for and more, much more, for it was there that I met the Autumn People.

Gran, my mother's mother, was my favourite person when I was little. I loved her best of all—I think I still do—and next to her came Jeanie.

Our home is on the coast of Pembrokeshire; our father, Evan Williams, is a dentist; our Scottish mother

writes thrillers; and Jeanie looks after us all. There are
five of us children: Sarah and Owen the two eldest, Alison and Chris younger, and I, Romilly, come right in the
middle.

With Gran I had a special relationship, and from the
age of seven my happiest times were when I went to stay
with her and Granda in London during my school holidays. Granda, who was Professor Robertson, spent most
of his time working in his lab at the University, so Gran
and I were often alone together; she liked to have me
with her, "to keep her company," she said.

Sometimes when it was wet and we couldn't go out,
Gran and I spent the day in her music room where her
piano was, and I played with her jewel box and her work
basket and then one day I was allowed to look at her old
photograph album—such funny old-fashioned-looking
people they were, and wearing such peculiar clothes.

There was a photograph of Gran as a little girl in a
white frilly dress and a floppy hat tied under her chin, and
white buttoned boots on her feet. She was holding the
hand of a lady whose skirts swept the ground, a lady in a
flat pancake hat tied on with a floating scarf.

"That is *my* mother, Romilly Graham," said Gran,
when I asked. "She was your great-grandmother whom
you are called after."

"*Am* I?" I cried entranced, staring at the haunting face
in the photograph. "Are we the only Romillies in the
family?"

"Yes, there are only the two of you," said Gran.

I sat on Gran's knee and rested the album on a table

before us, while she peered through her glasses at the fading photos, talking half to herself about the different family groups.

"Now those were taken on Karasay—here are the Graham cousins picnicking, and these are the Robertsons—Granda's family—look that's Granda with their first car; what an antique it looks! And here is Aunt Charlotte and some of the Graham cousins—and these are the Parsons, great friends of our family's. What wonderful times those were on Karasay, when we were all young and met there for the summer holidays every year!"

Together we laughed over the old photographs—Gran as a plump little girl with bobbing ringlets, Gran with her cousins in absurd sailors suits, Gran newly grown-up, her hair precariously piled on top of her head, Gran as a young bride on Granda's arm.

Later there were photos of Graham children, of my

mother and *her* cousins, a recurring pattern of family life.

But it was my namesake, my great-grandmother, the earlier Romilly, who interested me most, and I kept turning back to the pages where she appeared.

I was fascinated by the link between Gran's mother and me, a link that bridged almost a hundred years. "Tell me about her, about your mother," I begged. "Where did you live? Were you her favourite child?"

Patiently Gran answered my questions.

"I was her only child," she said. "We lived in Edinburgh in a house rather like this one, a tall thin house, set in a square of houses, built round a garden."

"And did you go to Karasay every summer? Where is Karasay?"

"It is an island off the north coast of Scotland," she said. "I used to go to stay there in the summer with my Graham cousins. Karasay House belonged to my grandfather, then to my Uncle Angus, and now my cousin, Derwent Graham, lives there with a cook and a housekeeper to look after him."

"Did you go there with your mother?" I asked.

"No, my mother hated the house and would never go back there even after she married my father, although she had stayed there as a girl; that's where they met one another. I never went to Karasay while my mother was alive," said Gran.

"How very strange!" I remarked. "Why did she hate it?"

"I don't know," Gran replied. "Something dreadful

happened while she was there, a tragedy; one of my uncles, Rodger Graham, disappeared. She would never talk about it."

"How d'you mean disappeared?" I asked.

"They thought he'd been swept away in a storm and drowned," Gran said. "It happened long before I was born."

I thought about this for a minute, then, "Tell me more about my great-grandmother," I begged. "What kind of person was she? Am I like her at all?"

"Yes, your features and colouring are very like hers, darling," said Gran, "but although she was my mother and I loved her dearly, I felt I never really knew her very well. She had a reserve, a quality of secretiveness, of aloofness, about her that often made me shy, even a little in awe, of her. I don't think she was a happy person, she had strange dark moods, though she could be gay at times. Of course, I was only a child of ten when she died."

"How sad!" I exclaimed. "And do you never go back to Karasay now?"

"I haven't for a long time. You see Granda likes to go abroad for holidays in the sun, or to climb in Switzerland," she explained, "but I *would* like to go there once again, and take you with me, Romilly."

"I'd like to see Karasay; I'd like it very much," I assured her.

After I discovered the photograph album, it became a game that we always played, Gran and I. The album was my storybook, the people were fairy-tale characters to me, and some of them I came to know quite well through the stories that Gran told me about them. It was a world I felt at home in, a pattern of life secure and orderly that appealed to me. I was able to identify myself with some of those old relations and friends of my great-grandmother's time, almost as if I belonged to their era. My games of make-believe were centred around them.

I never played with dolls or toy animals as most other children did. When I was not off in a corner dreaming, I played with paper and pencil, paints or fat crayons, drawing shapes or coloured patterns, designs rather than pictures. At Gran's I lay on the floor on my stomach, drawing, while Gran sat at the piano; she played a great deal and very well. When I think of those times I spent in Gran's music room I remember happiness.

I loved Gran's house; its order and tranquility delighted and satisfied me. The beautiful old furniture shone like satin and the furnishings filled me with pleasure. The curtains and chair covers in wonderful colours blossomed with flowers—exquisite, exotic, their leaves and stems intertwined in intricate patterns.

"They're the work of William Morris; there's no one like him," said Gran, and she certainly had been lavish with his designs about the house. I was fascinated by them because of my *own* passion for patterns, shapes. I saw them everywhere and I filled book after book with strange designs drawn in pencil or crayons.

Sarah laughed at me. "They're no good, they're too—odd, weird. Look, I'll show you what to draw," she said.

But from the start Gran encouraged me. "Stick to

your own ideas. They're unique and most original. If you work hard, you'll be an artist some day, a good one, and I shall be so proud of you," said Gran.

Next to Gran in my order of importance, came Jeanie. She was my friend and ally, she supported me in my quarrels with Sarah, she was my oracle, my rock in whose shelter my tender leaves sprouted. Our mother led a clever professional life, too busy for the everyday domesticities of her clutter of children. Our father was dedicated to his work and his boat. And although we knew that they loved us, it was Jeanie who coped with us all.

She came from the Scottish borders to work for Gran in London, but when our mother got married to our father and came to live in Pembrokeshire in Wales, Jeanie came with her, so we have known her all our lives; she has always been there.

Jeanie's cottage was a place of refuge to me when Sarah had driven me nearly to distraction. It was tiny and stood at the bottom of our garden. I loved its shining order, where each thing had its own place; its pattern of neatness gave me a feeling of well-being, of security. And there was the link with Gran, of course, which made Jeanie doubly important to me.

Sarah and I were opposites, our patterns of life quite different, but Sarah was not content to leave it at that; wildly untidy and disorganized herself, my tidiness seemed to nettle her into unkind teasing—"Victorian and pernickety," she called me. Not that I really cared. Nothing could have persuaded me to live in the chaos

with which Sarah surrounded herself. Luckily I didn't
have to, for Alison shared Sarah's room, and I had a tiny
slit of my own at the top of the house where I lived as I
wanted to.

Our house stands on the road with its back to the sea.
Before it the moors climb up to the sky, stretching for
miles and miles. Only sheep and mountain ponies wander
up there among the ground gorse and the heather and
climb over the strangely shaped outcrops of granite. And
curlews skim the patches of marsh, their haunting cry
rising from the reeds. I loved to climb up there myself, to
be alone, to lie in the heather and listen and think. Nobody bothered me up there; I could be my private self
and dream in peace.

There is a feeling of timelessness about the high moors
of Pembrokeshire, a sense of unbroken continuity, as if
little has changed in thousands of years. It is a primeval
land where the threads of ancient knowledge and prehistoric custom wind through to the present day. I sensed
this as I wandered alone and as I dreamed I felt the unseen presence of those who had been there before. It was
both frightening and comforting.

Jeanie says that like Scotland it has a special magic for
those who care to hear.

Jeanie is a believer in magic, in things unseen; her ear is
attuned to catch the whispered echoes from a world un-
heard by most. I was enchanted by this, for I sometimes
felt I knew as she did that there were powers we could
not always explain.

"I'm not blind or deaf to what's going on around me.

There's a power that can be felt, you know," she said.

"A power?" I queried. "What kind of power?"

"There's a power for good, but there is also a power for evil, a terrible power we do well to fear," she said, and shivered.

I was a little shaken to find that even the rocklike Jeanie had such secret fears; yet I knew some of her fears quite well—thunder, for example, she was terrified of.

Once I was caught by a thunder-storm on the beach below Jeanie's cottage and fled to her for shelter. She pulled me inside, bolted the door and took off my wet clothes to dry them at the fire, wrapping me in a tartan rug to keep me warm. Thunder clouds rolled nearer, darkening the sky, the room was flash-lit by lightning and an eerie wind sprang up and moaned in the chimney. I didn't mind the barrage of crashes overhead but Jeanie went white, threw herself on her knees and began to gabble something over and over again; a sort of prayer, I supposed, though I couldn't hear the words properly.

"What were you saying?" I asked her when the storm was over. "Tell me the words."

> "This ae nighte, this ae nighte,
> Every nighte and alle,
> Fire and sleet and candle-lyte
> And Christe receive thy saule," she muttered.

"Why do you say that?" I asked. "Is it a prayer?"

"Well, you could call it that," said Jeanie. "My grannie learnt me it. I always say it when I'm feart; it's kind of comforting."

A shiver ran up my spine; the words were fascinating, but to my ears they had a sinister ring, not a prayer surely but an incantation, or an exorcism perhaps?

When I got home I looked it up in the *Oxford Book of Verse;* "The Lyke-Wake Dirge," it was called. It was quite long and I read it aloud right through. "Used as a chant during the all-night wake or vigil kept over a corpse, a custom dating back to the Dark Ages," one dictionary informed me.

Its haunting words and rhythm appealed to me. I learned part of it by heart, and I wrote out the first verse in my best lettering and pinned it up in my room.

We lived a free and easy life out of school, going where we pleased, doing what we liked with a kind of abandon, which our parents encouraged—Jeanie was the one who disciplined us when we needed it.

In the summer Sarah and Owen went sailing with our father, but I got seasick and chose to stay at home. I played on the beach with Alison and Chris, making gardens in the sand and exploring the rock pools; then after a while I would wander off and climb one of the rocky headlands. There, tucked into a secret nook, I drew my patterns, which I took from the wild rock gardens of flowers around me, from the shapes of the little coloured fields across the bay, from the sunlight on the bright green prickles of the stubby young gorse, from the shadows of the gliding hawk.

One winter Granda had a bad heart attack, which kept

him a semi-invalid till his death three years later. During that time, of course, Gran would not leave him, for he preferred to stay quietly at home, so the long-planned visit to Karasay had to wait.

But after his death, when I was fifteen, we began to think again about going to Karasay in the summer.

By this time Sarah and Owen were sharing a flat in London, Sarah at art school and Owen working for extra 'A' levels.

I went around to see them several times, but there was a strangeness between me and them. We seemed to have lost contact with one another; they had moved into a different world and left me behind. The flat was chaotic and always crowded. I never did discover how many of their friends actually lived there. Nobody seemed to notice the mess and muddle or to think of cleaning or even of airing the rooms. Sarah looked me over with a critical eye and roused the old antagonism in me once again.

"You'll have to change a lot if you mean to come up to art school here," she remarked in a patronizing voice. "You're hopelessly . . . well . . . countrified and childish! You're simply not with it. But don't worry," she added more kindly, "I'll help you to get trendy; you'll soon learn to live as we all do and to dress properly— I'll teach you to find your way around when you're a bit older, Rom."

"Thanks, Sarah," I said, "but I don't think I want to change that much, only to grow up in my own way."

When I got back after the last visit to the flat, I talked to Gran about what I felt.

"Sarah seems to have got lost, caught up into this new way of living," I said, "and she expects me to follow her."

"Cheer up," said Gran, "you don't have to follow anyone; you'll make your own pattern, plan your own path. And don't worry about Sarah too much. I doubt if she has really changed basically; you and she have always been temperamentally different, haven't you? That doesn't prevent your being good friends, does it? It's better for each of you to go your own way, don't you think?"

"I suppose that's part of my trouble. I'm not sure yet which *is* my own way," I confessed.

"Aren't you?" Gran looked surprised. "*Aren't you?*" she repeated.

As the summer term dawdled on and the holidays came nearer, I began to look forward eagerly to going to Karasay.

There was a letter from Cousin Derwent in answer to Gran's, saying that he'd be delighted to have us. "There will be several young Grahams up here in August, Parsons too, so Romilly will have company of her own age."

I imagined myself in Karasay House with the Grahams who had once lived there. All those shadow people in the old photographs came sharply alive in my mind, and I remembered the stories Gran used to tell me about them. Particularly I thought of my namesake, my great-grandmother Romilly Carpentier who had become Romilly Graham. She fascinated and intrigued me. What had happened to her at Karasay? Why would she never go back to the house? Would I be able to discover the secret?

By the time school finished in the last week of July, I was all set to go. Gran was driving up the whole way from London to the north coast of Scotland, and we planned to spend several nights en route—but at the last minute I had a piece of rotten luck—I came down with mumps—badly, of course!

I raged and groaned and ached, but nothing could be done about it. I'd just have to wait until I was better, and then fly up to Karasay. Gran would have to go without me.

Jeanie looked after me and tried to cheer me up, but in spite of all her care and ministrations and remedies, the doctor would not let me travel till the very end of August.

"A month in the north of Scotland is just what you need, young woman," he said, "and you won't be going back to school till the end of September—that ought to please you!"

It did, and I took off at last, expectant and excited for my long-delayed visit to Karasay.

PART I

YESTERDAY: MILLIE

CHAPTER ONE

"But how can i go to stay with the Grahams? I don't know them, and I have no clothes, Mamma," I said, frowning.

"Don't be foolish, Millie, of course you must go; it's a wonderful chance for you to meet really nice people. As for your clothes, we'll manage somehow. Now take that sullen look off your face," she added, "and let's have no more of it."

My mamma wore her most determined expression, so I knew it was no use raising any more objections, besides it might be amusing to visit an outlandish island in the north of Scotland and to stay with well-to-do people. At least it would be a change from our wretchedly dull circumstances in London.

Mrs. Graham was a school friend of my mother's whom I had met once or twice on her visits to London, but her husband and family I did not know.

"Let me see now," continued Mamma, "Charlotte is a little younger than you, and there are three boys older,— Angus, Rodger and James—such a chance for the future, Millie dear."

"Whatever do you mean?" I said peevishly. "What chance? Why are you being so mysterious?"

"Come now, child, you are sixteen and must have a little more sense—a chance to marry well, later on of course, a chance to marry one of the Graham boys, you little goose!"

So that was it! I made a little grimace at Mamma; I would not let her rush me into matrimony. At the same time, marriage would be a solution to most of my problems. Since my mamma was a widow and we had very little money, my future was likely to be a bleak one, earning my own living as a governess, unless I were to marry into a well-to-do family; *then* I could lead the kind of life I longed for, a life of wealth with all the excitement I craved.

I made up my mind there and then to play my cards carefully, to get as much out of the Grahams as I could, now and in the future.

"Very well, I'll go," I agreed, "but I must have some new clothes, and what about the fare? It's a long way and it will be expensive."

My mother sighed. "We'll manage," she repeated, "but do make the most of your opportunities won't you? You can be so gay and charming when you care to be. The Graham family will enjoy having you to stay, if only you'll try to be at your most pleasant and do not show them the dark side of your nature, my dear."

She was obviously delighted at the invitation and went to her desk at once to write to Mrs. Graham. I followed her and stood beside her shoulder watching her begin her letter—

> *12 Leinster Terrace,*
> *London.*
> *June 10th, 1901*

My dear Grace,

> *What a delightful invitation for my little Millie! How very kind of you to think of such a treat for her. She will be charmed to spend July and August with you in your home on Karasay. It is most generous of you and your husband. Thank you for. . . .*

I grew bored and wandered off across the room, planning the wonderful clothes I would buy if only I had some money. I tried not to think of some of the things Mamma had said to me, especially about the dark side of my nature. I knew it was there. I tried to think that if only things were different for us, if we had more money and I had more clothes and more fun, I would not find

things in myself I did not really like. But I knew deep
down that that was not so. There were things in myself—
a deep hidden darkness—I did not understand. Maybe, I
thought, maybe a happy summer in another place would
help. And maybe a good marriage, a wealthy marriage,
was the answer. I resolved to see.

My mother and I worked hard renovating, repairing,
altering and remodelling my wardrobe. We even managed to afford to make one new dress. By the end of the
month I was fitted out and ready to set off on my adven-
ture.

It was a very long journey, and much to my annoyance
Mamma insisted on putting me in the charge of not only
the guard, but also an elderly lady travelling in the same
carriage. But after the first half hour, when I had answered all her questions, she fell asleep, and I was able to
do the same. I also had two books with me, and the time
passed quickly enough till I found myself at the little
port where I had to cross by boat to the island.

It was a smooth crossing, although it took three hours,
and then I saw ahead of me a group of islands, and we
made for the biggest of them. Soon we tied up and I
changed on to a smaller boat, which was waiting for us,
and immediately set sail for Karasay. We bounced across
the water for nearly another hour before we reached
Karasay and turned into its little harbour. It was busy
with fishing boats and other craft and gay with people
assembled on the quay to meet us. Mrs. Graham herself
was waiting for me and waved a welcome as soon as she
saw me. With her were one of her sons and a girl of

nearly my own age who could only be Charlotte.

Several pony traps and one open carriage were waiting by the quay, and when I stepped off the gangway Mrs. Graham came forward to kiss me, and after introducing Charlotte and Angus, she led the way to one of the pony traps.

"Bring Millie's trunk as quickly as you can, Angus," she called. "She must be dying to get into fresh clothes after her long journey. Well, my dear, it is very nice to have you safely here. Charlotte has been so excited about your visit. Tell me, how is your mother? I wish she and I could meet more often."

She chattered on while we waited, needing few answers from me, and presently Angus appeared with my small trunk on his shoulder, pretending to stagger under its weight. He lifted it into the trap, grinned at me and climbed into the driver's seat.

"Gee-up Marigold," he said, giving the reins a twitch, "but don't hurry yourself whatever you do!" Marigold began to saunter through the village at the pace that best suited her, slipping a little on the cobblestones, but no one paid any attention.

It seemed a very small village—only a tiny post office and general store combined, two or three other shops, a church, a little school and the "Fisherman's Safety Inn." There were quite a number of cottages with pretty gardens gay with flowers.

Soon we left the village, and as the road wound up the hill, between fields where everyone was out hay-making, Angus jumped down and took the pony's head. In a few

minutes Mrs. Graham pointed to a stone house ahead of
us. "That's Karasay House, our holiday home," she said,
"and this farmhouse we are passing now is Tallows
where our friends the Parsons come every summer.
You'll like the Parsons, Millie; there are three of them,
two boys and a girl, such handsome boys and such a
pretty little girl," she gushed. Angus gave a snort at this
point, which he turned into a cough that made Charlotte
giggle. We turned off the road and drove through a

white wooden gate, along a short drive and then stopped in front of the house. A wire fence with wooden posts ran all around it dividing the garden from the fields, and on some of the posts, hunched and sinister, sat brooding some of the biggest rooks I had ever seen.

A young maid in a black frock and a starched white cap and apron stepped briskly from the house and came to take Mrs. Graham's shopping and my hand luggage; she beamed a welcome to me in a most friendly manner.

"Take Miss Millie up to her room, Catha, and see that she has everything she wants; then you can bring tea out on to the terrace," said Mrs. Graham.

"Yes ma'am," said Catha; then turning to me, "This way please, Miss."

"I'll bring your trunk up in a minute," Angus called after me as I followed Catha up the stairs. My room was small, very neat and plain with a sloping roof and a window facing inland across the garden. There was a polished floor, and the counterpane of the bed was white. A glass of wild flowers stood beside the candle on the bedside table. Behind it on the wall hung a framed text, "Thou God see-est me." On the marble-topped wash-stand inside a china basin stood a brass can of hot water covered with a towel.

"I hope you had a good journey, Miss," said Catha. "It must be a long way to come from London. Have you got everything you need? The bathroom is across the passage, and Miss Charlotte's room is on one side of you, Mr. Rodger's on the other."

Before I could answer her, there was a loud stamping

on the stairs and Angus arrived with my trunk.

"Here you are," he said, dumping it at the bottom of the bed. "What have you got in it—the crown jewels? It feels heavy enough!"

"All my belongings for two months," I replied primly. I did not like being teased.

"Shall I help you to unpack, Miss?" Catha offered when he had gone, but I shook my head. I did not want Catha to see how meagre were my belongings, how few my clothes.

"No thank you, Catha, I can manage quite easily," I said.

"Very well, Miss; tea will be ready in half an hour. Shall I ask Miss Charlotte to come and fetch you?"

"Oh yes, that would be kind, thank you," I said, and I knelt to unlock the trunk.

I washed my hands and face in the soft brown water and changed my dress, then I took down my hair which I had worn piled on the top of my head for the journey to make me look older. I brushed it out and tied it in a bunch with a piece of velvet ribbon, and I tucked the odd straggling wisps away with hairpins. By the time Charlotte knocked at my door I had stowed my underclothes away in the drawers, and hung my dresses and skirts in the wardrobe and arranged my two hats on a shelf.

Charlotte peeped in rather shyly.

"Are you ready, Millie?" she asked. "Is there anything I can get for you? No? Then come, and I'll take you down to tea. Oh!" she confided, slipping her hand into mine as we walked down the stairs together, "I'm so glad you've come to stay, it's awful being the only girl in the house! You mustn't mind Angus teasing you, he and James are really very kind." She paused a moment and I wondered why she did not include Rodger. "I do hope you are going to like it here?" she added.

"I'm sure I am," I responded. "It is wonderful to get away from London and to live in a family, and so kind of your parents to invite me."

Charlotte's warm friendliness and obvious admiration had already begun to work on me. I had not expected to find her so endearing. I thought suddenly that it would be easy here, as I had hoped, to be the happy person I could be.

She smiled and took my arm as we crossed the hall and approached the terrace, which we could see through an open door.

"Come along my dears," said Mrs. Graham, motioning us to chairs near the tea table. Mr. Graham rose and held out his hand to me. "Welcome, Miss Millie," he said, "we are very glad to have you with us. Angus you already know; Rodger, James, this is Millie Carpentier."

Involuntarily I caught my breath and put out a hand to steady myself as the two young men came forward to welcome me. Never had I seen anyone so startlingly, alarmingly handsome as Rodger, and as I sat down I lowered my eyes in confusion, transfixed by his dark compelling gaze.

CHAPTER TWO

HE WAS A MOST EXTRAORDINARY BOY, DARK AND INTELLI-
gent with a dynamic quality about him, an irresistible
magnetism. His eyes were brilliant and black as coal—
black not brown. I felt drawn to him, excited by him,
and at the same time repelled, for there was something
about him that caused an instinctive shudder. Somehow
he made red-headed Angus and James with his fresh
open face seem insignificant.

All through tea time as we chatted politely I felt his
attention focused on me; he plied me with food and
watched for my teacup to empty, but he never spoke a
word, yet I felt he knew exactly what I was thinking. I

was glad when tea time came to an end. I had found it quite an ordeal, for Rodger never took his eyes off me, and it was impossible to tell whether he was pleased with me or not, whether his eyes were admiring or contemptuous. His preoccupation with me had a curious effect on his family. Charlotte drew her chair closer to me, James came over and sat behind me, and Angus kept up an amiable chatter; only Mr. and Mrs. Graham seemed oblivious of the strange atmosphere in the room.

At last James suggested that Charlotte and he show me the garden, and asked Mrs. Graham's permission to leave the table.

The garden was quite large and was hidden from the road by a stone wall, which protected the herbaceous borders of flowers from the wind. We strolled along the paved path, Charlotte holding my arm, till we reached a little terraced alcove containing a tiny summer-house, which looked onto a croquet lawn.

"Shall we play?" asked James, indicating the mallets and balls.

"If you wish," I replied, hoping to please him.

"No, let's sit here and talk," said Charlotte. "Let's get to know one another."

So we sat down, the three of us, and they questioned me about my life in London, about school and home, about my mother and my friends, but all so gently and with such real interest that I lost my reserve and spoke frankly.

"Now it's my turn," I said after a while. "There are lots of things I want to know about all of you."

I learned that Angus was nineteen and in his second
year of medicine at Edinburgh University; James was
seventeen, a year older than myself; and Charlotte two
years younger than I.

"And Rodger?" I asked.

"Eighteen," said James shortly. "He has just left
school."

"And what is he going to do?" I asked.

James shrugged his shoulders. "Only Rodger knows
that," he said. "Tomorrow, Millie, you must meet our
friends the Parsons," he continued, changing the subject.
"They're away for the day today. They come up here
every summer holiday just as we do. Theirs is the farmhouse just across the road from us."

"Tell me about them," I suggested.

"Well, there's Jocelyn the eldest; he's eighteen and
just finished school; then Robert who's my age; and little
Janetta who is only twelve."

"And do they live in Edinburgh too?"

"Oh no, their home is in London, but Mr. Parsons and
our father were at the University together and have been
friends ever since."

Suddenly I began to yawn and tried to smother it, but
Charlotte noticed and jumped up at once.

"Millie, how stupid of me, you must be feeling very
tired after your journey, and we have kept you chatter-
ing here! You must come and lie down till dinner time; a
sleep is what you need. I'll come with you to your
room."

When I had taken off my dress and slipped in between

the sheets I realized how tired I was, and knowing that Charlotte would waken me in good time to dress for dinner, I fell into a deep sleep.

I was wakened by a knocking on the door, and Charlotte came in followed by Catha with another can of hot water.

"Are you feeling rested a little?" Charlotte asked. "You have plenty of time before dinner. Can I help you to dress?"

"Stay if you like and help me to put my hair up," I suggested. "Mamma said I should wear it up in the evenings."

"Oh yes, let me brush it for you when you are ready. You've got lovely long silky hair, Millie; I wish my rat-tails were more like it."

I decided to wear my new dress. I wanted to make a good impression on my first evening, and Charlotte was full of admiration as she fastened it up the back for me. It was made of spotted muslin and was trimmed with bows and bands of blue velvet. I hoped it made me look older, especially when I wore my hair up.

Dinner was a very leisurely meal and lasted for nearly an hour and a half, there were so many different courses.

Charlotte told me afterwards that it was only when her governess was on holiday and they were at Karasay, or when the boys were at home, that she was allowed to have dinner with her parents instead of supper in the schoolroom, and I thought how different was my life alone with my mother.

All through dinner I noticed Rodger watching me, and

even when his eyes were turned in the opposite direction
I felt that he was aware of everything about me. It was
disturbing but also exciting.

When dinner was over a game of cards till bedtime
was suggested, but I made the excuse that I wanted to
write to Mamma before I went to sleep and asked leave
to go to my room.

It was not yet dark but the lamps were already lit, and
James came with me into the hall to light a candle for me
to take upstairs.

When I reached my room, I found the curtains drawn,
the sheets of the bed turned down and my nightgown
laid out by the pillow. I lit the candle by my bed, and sat
down at the little desk with a candle on each side of me
to write my letter to my mother. I felt confused with so
many new impressions, but I told her that I liked the
Graham family, especially James and Charlotte, and that
I thought my stay would be a pleasant one. I meant it.

Rodger I did not mention in my letter, I had not quite
sorted out my thoughts about him. I brushed my hair
and plaited it for the night, and long after I got into bed,
I lay in the darkness thinking about him, disturbed by his
lean secretive face with its mocking expression, an old-
young face, shadowed and knowing.

The next morning James and Charlotte decided to ar-
range a picnic for the afternoon and I went with them to
invite the Parsons. They all agreed to come except Jocelyn who was visiting friends for a few days, so I did not
meet him.

"Will Angus or Rodger be coming to the picnic?"

little Janetta asked. "I like Angus *very* much."

"Oh, Angus will come, I expect," said James, "but not Rodger I shouldn't think, he hardly ever comes on family expeditions."

"Too busy with his photography I suppose," said Robert. "I must say he's very good; his animal photographs are excellent."

So Rodger was interested in animal photography—I was surprised; I had not thought him capable of enough patience.

To everyone's surprise Rodger decided to come. "He must be fascinated by you, Millie," Charlotte teased me. I felt complimented, but at the same time I fervently hoped her words were not true. I had rather Rodger kept his distance from me.

We set off for the picnic in the Parsons' wagonette, but the boys went ahead on their bicycles, taking little Janetta with them. The chosen place was a sheltered bay protected from the wind by a little wood. The boys bathed but the water was considered too cold for the girls who had to be content with tucking up their skirts and paddling in the shallows.

Soon sticks were collected and a fire started, and before long the kettle boiled and a splendid tea was spread out—we were all ravenous.

Charlotte sat down on one side of me, James on the other, in the middle of the group of picnickers, but I was painfully aware of Rodger sitting opposite me, his mocking gaze fixed once again on me. Consequently I felt horribly self-conscious and could not enjoy my tea.

When we had finished eating we young people dashed
to the wood and a riotous game of hide and seek began.

James was "it," and I ran to hide behind a rock on the
far edge of the trees. I waited there panting while James
finished counting aloud. Suddenly without a sound arms
came fiercely round me from behind, pinioning mine to
my sides. I got such a fright I opened my mouth and
screamed, "James! Save me, save me!"

"You little fool," hissed Rodger as he let me go, "don't
tell."

When James came bounding toward the rock crying,
"Millie! Whatever is wrong?" Rodger had vanished so I
made a lame excuse. "I think I saw . . . an adder," I
stammered. "I cannot abide snakes!"

James took my arm and comforted me and led me
back to Mrs. Graham and I was made to sit down and
was fussed over by the grown-ups while the game went
on.

No apology came from Rodger; in fact he avoided me
for the rest of the evening. What had been his intention?
To frighten me, to excite me, to draw my attention to
himself, to demonstrate his strength? I simply could not
tell. Perhaps he was just showing off.

I wished he would leave me alone. I was frightened of
his attraction for me for I felt that his appeal was to the
darkness in myself that I wished to keep hidden, that I
wished to lose.

CHAPTER THREE

AFTER THE FIRST FEW DAYS I BEGAN TO FEEL QUITE ESTAB-
lished and settled in the Graham household, and as I had
hoped, I found myself enjoying it all very much. It was
delightful to be the guest of such kind and friendly
people, and I revelled in the luxury of being waited upon
and made much of. After the rather isolated life I led in
London, it was exciting to be in the same house as three
young men—no wonder Charlotte remarked that my
eyes had begun to sparkle.

Usually I was shy and withdrawn before strangers,
but the Graham family disarmed me with their genuine
kindness and affection; they had taken me straight to

their hearts. It was easy to be charming and gay with people I liked so much, who appreciated me and found me attractive. I felt ashamed that I could ever have planned to use them for my own ends. All I now wanted was to become like them, to belong to their group; to follow their way of life was my pleasure and my security.

They were an easy affectionate family, uncomplicated in their relationships with one another, although Rodger was the odd one out, and a puzzling person. They all seemed nervous of him and tried to keep on his right side, so that I wondered if he had a violent temper or suffered from some hidden ailment that made them indulgent toward him. He deliberately isolated himself, working away on his own in the old wash house, developing and printing his negatives, they said, or stalking over the hills or out on the cliffs, taking his animal photographs, which everyone said were so wonderful, but which I had not seen.

He made me uncomfortable and I tried to avoid ever being alone with him by keeping Charlotte or James constantly near me, but I did not always succeed. Even when Rodger was not actually with me I felt myself watched and threatened.

One shining morning when the dew was heavy on the grass and the haze of promised heat veiled the sun, I got up early and went out into the garden. Mrs. Graham had asked me to cut some flowers for the house before the sun was up. I had collected quite a sizable bunch when I decided to gather some of the tall feathery grasses that grew along the sides of the drive. Gradually I worked

my way down to the gate, absorbed in what I was doing.

"Good morning!"—the clear voice startled me and I looked up. Across the road leaning over the wall of the Parsons land stood a tall young man in a Norfolk jacket. "You must be the charming Miss Millie I've been hearing so much about," he said, smiling down on me.

"And you . . . must be Jocelyn Parsons," I replied in an unsteady voice, and my heart began to race with pleasure before his smiling glance. Jocelyn jumped the wall and strolled lazily across to me, holding out his hand. "Let me carry those flowers for you," he offered, and I handed them over to him.

We wandered up the drive to the house, and I was delighted just to be with him. The Graham family were grouped on the doorstep and called out good morning and invited Jocelyn to breakfast. But he refused and with a quick glance in my direction he was gone. As I entered the house Rodger stepped back into the shadow, and I caught on his face a look of fury. Evidently he resented the attention Jocelyn had paid me.

I would have to be careful in the future not to rouse his jealousy, to keep my face shuttered when Rodger was about, for I was determined to see as much of Jocelyn as possible.

Devoted as I was to the Graham family, I began to spend some of my time over at Tallows where there was no Rodger to embarrass and frighten me; not that he did or said anything—it was the way he looked at me. He was constantly in my mind and I could not forget him. There was certainly something very strange about him, a quality I can only describe as a dark power, which both fascinated and repelled me. I began to find Karasay House oppressive, uneasy, overshadowed by him, and there were times when I had to escape to Tallows to keep my peace of mind.

At Tallows I felt safe, cherished and protected by the affection of the whole Parsons family, and gradually Jocelyn and I got to know one another as our liking grew, first into something deeper, and then into love. I was left in no doubt that he cared for me as much as I did for him, although he did not declare his love. Daily we grew closer to one another and his parents came to accept me as a prospective daughter, while the Grahams looked on with approval. I did not mention Jocelyn in any of my letters to my mother. The whole situation was too new to me, too wonderful to write about. I wanted to keep it secret. I had never been in love before. My mother would have been delighted; it was what she would have described as a good match, although the thought of Jocelyn's money, his inheritance, hardly came into it. I loved him for himself and I'd have loved him had he been penniless.

I had usually been able to avoid being alone with Rodger but now that changed. He began to waylay me, to pursue me.

One morning I offered to go to the quay for Mrs. Graham to buy the fish for lunch when the catch was landed. Charlotte had already gone over to Tallows so I set off down the hill alone. I came to the village then to the quay where the fish were laid out for sale. I made my selection, paid for it, put the parcel into my basket and turned to go, but the basket was taken from my hand and when I looked up Rodger stood before me.

"I've been waiting for you, Millie," he said quietly.

I was taken by surprise and was quite at a loss how to escape from him. I had no wish for his company all the way back to Karasay House.

"I have to call at the post office," I began. "It may take some time if. . . ."

"I'm in no hurry," he replied. "We'll go together."

I had not brought my own purse and had only a few

pennies in my pocket but I went inside and bought stamps for my letters home, delaying as long as I could before rejoining Rodger. He was there on the doorstep waiting for me, and we started up the hill together. When we reached the first bend in the road, a farm boy mounted on a cart horse came clattering down the hill raising the dust and scattering the loose stones on the road. One of them hit Rodger on the ankle.

Rodger turned on him furiously. "Curse you!" he cried, "keep to your side of the road!" Immediately, as if he had been stung, the great horse reared up on his hind legs, tossed the boy off his back, and then galloped on down the hill. The boy lay on the road, his breath driven out of him by the fall, his face white, his head bleeding and bruised.

Horrified I ran to him and helped him to his feet, brushing the dust off him with my hand and pressing my handkerchief to the cut on his head.

"Are you all right?" I asked. "Are you hurt? Rodger! Come and help him!" But Rodger, whistling, walked on up the hill unconcernedly.

The boy grinned at me. "My Grannie's cottage is just down the road," he said. "Thanks, Miss, I can manage fine." Then he turned and glared at Rodger.

"The devil take you, Rodger Graham!" he shouted. "Ye'll come to a bad end."

When I caught up with Rodger, shocked at what I'd seen, I was also very angry.

"What a beastly thing to do!" I cried. "That boy might have been badly hurt and it would have been your fault!" Then as the strangeness of the incident struck me, "*How* did you frighten the horse?" I asked. Rodger just turned and looked at me but his secret smile sent shivers up my spine. The whole thing struck me as most peculiar, uncanny almost, and when we came to Tallows I made an excuse to go and find Charlotte, and so escaped from him.

A few days later another curious thing happened, again connected with Rodger, again nightmarish and inexplicable, and it happened to Catha, of whom I was very fond.

I had gone to my room after tea and was sewing a fresh lace collar and cuffs onto the dress I meant to wear for dinner that evening. The door was slightly open, the window wide as I sat stitching.

"How many times must I tell you to leave my room alone!" Rodger's curt words came clearly along the corridor.

"I'm sorry, Mr. Rodger, I was only putting up your clean curtains as the mistress ordered," I heard Catha reply.

"I won't have you poking about in my room. I don't like it; I've told you before. This time you'll have to be punished."

"Oh no, please not, Mr. Rodger, please don't punish me." Catha sounded really upset and I hated Rodger for bullying the girl. I heard her hurry past my door and run downstairs. Then a moment later I saw her cross the back green and begin to unpeg the washing from the line. Next she went to pick up the tablecloths that were bleaching on the grass—then I heard her scream. I threw down my sewing and ran. Mrs. MacCrindle, the cook, reached her first and I saw her put her arms around the frightened girl, soothing and comforting her.

"It bit me—an adder bit me!" Catha sobbed. "I thought it was a stick lying on the cloth—and when I picked it up, it bit my hand. Horrible! Look!"

A blue mark like a crescent moon showed on the fleshy part at the base of her thumb. I held her by the wrist and helped to lead her toward the house. She was badly shaken.

"I've been punished you see," Catha whispered to me as Mrs. Graham came hurrying toward us.

I stared at the girl, horrified. Rodger couldn't have done this? It wasn't possible . . . and yet. . . .

"Better get her to the doctor at once, ma'am," said Mrs. MacCrindle.

"I'll take her, and I'll find James to drive us," I offered, and I ran to the house.

Catha was back at work next morning, her hand bound up. Everyone was very kind to her and she seemed to have quite recovered her poise. These two incidents shocked me terribly. I was unable to find any logical explanation of how Rodger could have been responsible for them, yet I could not help feeling that he had. I knew they hated him in the village, and I began to see why.

One evening as I ran up to my room for more embroidery thread, I found him waiting for me at the top of the stairs. I had spent the afternoon with Jocelyn in the garden of Tallows, and my happiness spilled over so that I felt myself glowing with it. Even Rodger's daunting face did not at first destroy it.

"There is something I must say to you, Millie," he began, "a warning I must ask you to take very seriously. Jocelyn Parsons is not for you; you must give him up, unless you wish him harm."

There was something so horrible and sinister about his threat, especially when I remembered what had happened to Catha and to the farm boy, that I was filled with alarm and foreboding. I turned and fled from him in a panic, down the stairs through the open door, out along the drive, straight to the Parsons' house. I burst through the door and threw myself into Mrs. Parsons' arms.

"Why Millie, my dear, whatever is the matter?" she cried, drawing me into the room where the rest of the family were sitting. They clustered round me solicitous and concerned, trying to soothe and comfort me and to discover what had frightened me so. I clung to Jocelyn's hand, drawing strength from it, and soon I stopped trembling and recovered my self-control. I did not tell them about Rodger because I was afraid to, but I made an excuse to account for my fright, and later Jocelyn took me back to Karasay House.

For a few days nothing happened. I was almost able to forget Rodger's threat, at least to put it to the back of my mind. I saw Jocelyn every day and we kept out of Rodger's sight, making the most of our private world of delight.

It was the happiest time of my life, those weeks on

Karasay, in spite of Rodger and my anxieties and fears because of him. Since my father's early death, my mother and I had had a grim struggle to make ends meet. Money was very scarce and there was little left over for luxuries, but on Karasay the Grahams and Parsons lived in ease and comfort, and in what seemed like luxury to me. No wonder that I appreciated and enjoyed it to the full; no wonder that my kind hosts drew out the best in me so that I responded with a spontaneous affection I did not know was in me. My mother would not have recognized me. I found myself bubbling over with enjoyment, and anxious to give what pleasure I could with both hands.

The dream was too wonderful to last, and when it broke, my happiness shattered into a thousand pieces.

Day after day of sunshine and blue skies had parched the land to tawny tones, the roads were deep in dust and water was scarce, but then one day we could feel a change was coming. The fishermen shook their heads and predicted a break in the weather.

The day had been sultry and overcast, and by evening the air was so oppressive that we knew a storm must soon break.

Mr. and Mrs. Graham had gone out to dine with neighbours, so after our meal Angus, James, Charlotte and I settled to a game of cards. But as I grew more and more restless and could not concentrate, I excused myself and took my embroidery to a chair by the window. The game broke up, the boys went off to fiddle with their fishing rods, and Charlotte sat down beside me. The room was suffocating and when Charlotte began to yawn I suggested that she should leave me and go to bed.

"I did want to wait up with you till Papa and Mamma got back," she said, "but if you don't mind being left, Millie, I think I'll say good night."

"Good night; I'll follow you very soon," I said, as she kissed me.

I began to think of Jocelyn and to long to see him just for a few minutes; to hear his voice, to touch his hand. Dare I walk through the dusky garden across the road to Tallows, or was it too late for such a call? Perhaps Jocelyn too felt restless and had a longing for me; perhaps we would meet in the garden, or on the drive, if I slipped out quickly now—

I stepped out of the open window into the garden. The night was sultry and scented and very still but I heard the growl of approaching thunder. From the wash house a light shone out and I thought that Rodger was safely occupied with his photography. I crossed the lawn and followed the path to the empty summerhouse, then on through the little wood and out to the road. But there was no sign of Jocelyn and the storm was coming nearer. I had better get safely indoors before it broke.

I turned and doubled back toward the house, then paused a moment in the wood as a fantastic flash of lightning lit the trees—and at that moment a shrill terrified scream rose piercingly into the air. It came from quite close by, the tortured cry of an animal in pain. I searched around me, bending, poking in the undergrowth, afraid of finding something trapped, mangled, but compelled to

try to help. I found instead a large hole in the bank behind me, hidden by a fallen log and trailing creepers, and
as I knelt to look more closely, the scream, feebler this
time, came again from inside the hole. I hesitated, dread-
ing to make my way in till I came to I knew not what
horror, but just then there was a loud crash of thunder
and such a deluge of torrential rain that I was forced to
take shelter inside the hole. Crouched in the entrance I
grew bolder and began to crawl in, feeling my way along
a sort of tunnel. After a few moments I came to a bend,
and around it I was astonished to see a glow of light
ahead of me. I went forward more quickly then, as another scream urged me on. There before me I saw, silhouetted against the candlelight, the figure of a youth,
his head bent over something he held in his hands above
the flame—it was Rodger! There was a horrible smell of
burning and repeated weak cries—appalled I realized
what he was doing. In a passion of rage I hurled myself
out of the tunnel.

"Stop it!" I yelled. "You brute! Stop it at once!" I
sprang across the floor at him, meaning to batter him
with my bare fists till he let the creature he held go, if it
was still capable of going.

I took him completely by surprise, and as he jumped
back from the flame, his expression was one of utter in-
credulity.

"How on earth did you find your way in here?" he
gasped. "Nobody knows about this place, nobody but
me."

Then his face darkened with anger. "How *dare* you

come in here without being invited?" he demanded. I thought he was going to hit me, and I put up my arm to shield my face and stepped back toward the tunnel. He caught me by the wrist and dragged me forward again, and I noticed his hand was cold as ice. There was a scuffling noise across the floor as the little animal he had been torturing escaped to safety. We stood facing one another. I was panting with rage, my eyes blazing with anger. "You devil!" I exploded. "You cruel cold devil!"

He chuckled appreciatively. "I like to see you roused, my dear; there's a devil in you too—it's part of your appeal."

I tried to wrench myself from his grasp, but he was too quick for me.

"Oh no, you don't get away so easily, my dear Millie," he said. Keeping hold of my wrist he pulled me across the floor, kicked a kind of lever in the wall with his foot, and a great slab of stone swung down into place, shutting off the tunnel, shutting us in.

"Have a good look around," he invited. "You might like to see for yourself some of my . . . interests, shall we say?"

Curious, I looked around me; we were in a rough underground chamber hewn from the rock. The floor was polished smooth but the roof was jagged with great splinters of rock that looked as if they might fall at any moment. It had been a quarry at one time, and I supposed there must be a hidden air shaft leading up through the rock to the daylight. In the centre of the room was a stone table on which stood the candle, a black iron pot

and various jars and bottles containing different substances. Behind the table, neatly arranged on stone
shelves along the wall, I saw, gleaming whitely, a dozen
or more skeletons of small animals. They were grotesque
and twisted and I felt sickened and savage with anger as
I remembered the cries that had brought me into the
place. The air stank of burning, of animal, of damp, of
horror; I found it nauseating. On the walls at the dim
edges of the kindly circle of candlelight there hung the
dried pelts of many small creatures, some bunches of
herbs, a fox's mask and brush. On the far corner of the
table there were several miniature human figures made of
clay, and beyond them in the dark corners of the room I
sensed the shadows of evil, of witchcraft. I did not dare
to look again.

At last, I knew the truth about Rodger. It was worse
than anything I could have imagined. I shrank away
from him and tried to drag myself free.

"Are there others like you on the island?" I asked.

"Oh yes, there are others who practise witchcraft, but
I have nothing to do with them. This place is known to
me alone. I prefer my own company—I always have—
and sometimes yours, Millie."

"And no one, neither your parents nor your family,
suspects what you really are?"

"No, how could they?" said Rodger, "They are on one
side of the veil, and I on the other. They are incapable of
understanding me. They are innocents, you see, but they
have learned to accept my eccentricities without probing
too deeply." I began to understand at last the family's

attitude to him, which had puzzled me ever since I met them.

"Well, now you know," he said quietly, tightening his hold on my wrist, "what are you going to do about it?"

There was a hint of triumph in his voice that made me realize I was completely at his mercy. I looked around me hoping wildly for a miracle to happen, but I was trapped, helpless; there was no escape from this place. I longed for Jocelyn, for Angus, James, *anyone* to come to my rescue, but how could they? No one knew where I was, buried under the earth.

"You're perfectly right, no one will hear you if you scream," said Rodger, reading my thoughts. "We are deep in the rock and my portcullis is lowered—no one can get in or out."

"You're mine, Millie, mine to do what I like with. Get down on your knees, you're *my* creature."

I struck at him with my free hand but he dodged the blow and pulled me forward onto my knees.

He stood looking down on me, gloating; his cold hand stroked my cheek, then he bent and kissed me and I spat in his face.

"You shouldn't have done that," he said softly. "You'll have to pay for it you know." I felt sick with rage and disgust. "Come now, you want to get out of here alive, don't you," he continued. "No one would ever find you if I left you here; nobody knows of this place except me, so you'd better promise at once to do as I say; to obey me now and always." My heart sank in despair. I knew he meant it.

CHAPTER FOUR

I FELT I HAD BEEN SHUT UP WITH RODGER FOR HOURS, BUT
in reality it could not have been for more than a few
minutes. I wondered if the rain had stopped, if any one
had missed me, but I was sure they'd think I had gone to
bed and no one would discover I was missing till Catha
brought my tea and can of hot water in the morning.
Somehow I had to satisfy Rodger, to promise him
enough to secure my release, although I had no intention
of *keeping* any promise made under such compulsion.

But I had underestimated his cunning; he was too
clever for me. As I rose to my feet to confront him, to
bargain with him, he forced me down onto my knees

again, and while still holding me by the wrist he whipped out his pocketknife and opened it with his teeth. I thought he was going to kill me.

"You have brought this on yourself through blundering in here," he said. "I have had no time to prepare you for your role—I have chosen you to be my disciple; I am your master. I marked you from the start, ever since I saw you, you have the capacity to be a part of this, but I had planned to wait for a little, for a year or two until I married you before I initiated you into the mysteries of my craft. You have only yourself to blame for changing my plans, so you must put up with shock treatment and do as I say—or remain here for good. Now—promise, *swear*, that you will never, never under any circumstance, no matter what happens, tell any living person of the existence of this place, or what you have seen here."

"I promise," I said quietly, "but only if *you* promise never again to bring any living creature into this . . . chamber of horror."

"Well-tried, my dear Millie, but it won't do."

Suddenly his face turned vicious, and he showed his teeth like an animal—like a fox—and with a swift movement he drew the thin blade of his knife first across the inside of my wrist, then of his own, where there was a scar, like a brand mark on his skin which I had not noticed before. I thought he must be mad.

"Now promise again and mean it," he said, "or do I have to brand you to show you I'm in deadly earnest?" I looked at the blood slowly oozing out of the cuts and then at Rodger's implacable face, and I shuddered.

"And make no mistake," he added, "if you break your promise *in any way*, Jocelyn Parsons will be the first one to suffer, I'll see to that."

It was the final blow and it broke me. I was helpless, trapped; I daren't *not* keep any promise I made. I dared not risk Jocelyn being harmed, for I believed that Rodger was capable of anything. I remembered again with a new kind of horror how he had cursed the boy on the cart horse, and his threat of punishment to Catha; how could I doubt his power to harm Jocelyn?

"Very well, I promise," I muttered, and this time he knew I meant it unconditionally.

"Repeat after me—I, Romilly Carpentier, do solemnly swear to keep the promise of silence I have made to Rodger Graham." Unwillingly I repeated his words.

Then he surprised me by placing his cut wrist against mine so that our blood mingled. It was ludicrous and childish, yet under those circumstances and in that place it was both frightening and impressive.

"You're mine, Millie," he exulted, and the triumph in his voice sickened me. "You're mine, now and forever."

He pulled me quite gently to my feet and led me to the stone table. From there he selected a jar and rubbed some kind of ointment onto my wound, and then he bound it with my handkerchief.

"The cut will soon heal," he assured me, "and if any-one remarks on it you must say you tore your wrist on a thorn."

He seemed elated, excited, and in a strangely good humour as if he had achieved something of merit. I waited wondering what he would do next before he let me go. Anxiously I watched him unbutton his shirt and take off a slim chain that he wore around his neck from which hung a little ring of stone. He undid the chain, took the ring off and pushed it onto my finger.

"You can go now," he said abruptly, "but remember you are *mine*, and I will be watching you."

He wound up the stone door slab, and I stumbled dazedly across the floor and bolted into the tunnel like a scared rabbit. The rain was still very heavy when I got outside but I paid no attention to it. I was so thankful to be out in the sweet fresh air again that I took in great gulps of it, as slithering and stumbling I dashed for the house. There seemed to be nobody about as I let myself in, although the lamps were still lit. Thankfully I crept up the stairs and reached my room unobserved. I locked the door, struggled out of my sodden clothes and filled the basin with hot water from the can. I saw to my amazement that it was barely ten o'clock, less than an hour since I had left the drawing room, yet in that short space of time I felt my whole life had been changed.

Carefully I sponged the wound on my wrist, then I washed myself all over, every single inch of me. I thought I could never feel clean again. Exhausted I crawled into bed at last and the full horror of my experience flooded over me. My teeth began to chatter and my body to shudder, as I struggled to put the whole thing out of my mind. I slept fitfully, dreaming horribly, starting awake at every sound, and when the morning finally came I lay still, exhausted.

Two certainties emerged from the night's turmoil: I had to protect Jocelyn by keeping my promise of silence, and I had to keep out of Rodger's way, give him no chance to use his dangerous power over me. I must resist and fight him with everything I had. I was convinced, however silly it may sound, that he had put me under a spell, that he could compel me to do his will, that a part of me would follow him if I let down my guard, that he was evil and corrupt himself, and that there was no escape from him.

I glanced up at the text over my bed and I felt it should read, "Thou, Rodger, seest me."

I knew that the wisest thing I could do was to make some excuse to Mrs. Graham and go home at once, but that would mean leaving Jocelyn and I could not do it. I had to stay.

Soon I heard stirrings in the house and I got up and unlocked my door for I knew that Catha would soon be coming with my hot water and my tea.

From the landing window I could see that it was a lovely clear morning after the storm; the sea and sky merged in an all-over blueness, and a magical light pinpointed the neighbouring islands. But my spirits did not soar with the beauty of the summer day. I felt myself enclosed in darkness, in a shadow I could not shake off. I could not forget Rodger or what had happened in his horrible hiding place under the ground. At least I could rid myself of his ring. I suppose I had been too shocked to think of it sooner, but now I wrenched it off my finger and looked around for a suitable place to hide it. I wished never to see it again. There were spaces between the floorboards where the old wood had warped or shrunk, surely a safe place for losing something best hidden and forgotten. I dropped the stone ring down one of the spaces out of sight. I felt better then, as if by discarding his ring I had been able to throw off part of his hold over me.

When Catha arrived, tapping discreetly on the door so as not to waken me suddenly, she found me sitting up in bed. She looked at my pile of drenched clothes on the floor and then at me.

"Oh *Miss!*" she exclaimed. "Were you caught in the storm last night? Oh, poor Miss, you must have been soaked. I'll take your clothes away with me now. Is there

anything else I can get you?"

"No thank you, Catha, you're very kind. A cup of tea is just what I need, and then I'll have a bath."

"Shall I bring your breakfast to you in bed then, Miss? You look really out of sorts this morning, and no wonder. Perhaps you've caught a chill?"

"I think I'll get up, thank you, Catha," I said. "I thought I heard someone at the bottom of the garden last night and went out to investigate, and the rain caught me. But I'm all right now," I lied glibly. I had to give some explanation of my sodden garments; no one must guess the truth.

When I got downstairs I found I could not eat any breakfast. My head ached and I felt so shivery that Mrs. Graham took me back to my room and insisted on my spending the day in bed.

"Catha tells me you were caught in the rain last night!" she exclaimed. "Whatever were the boys thinking of to let you go out alone?"

"No one saw me go," I replied, "and it wasn't for long."

"Long enough to make you ill," said Mrs. Graham. "Now try to go to sleep, my dear, and if you are not better tomorrow I will send for the doctor. You don't look feverish so I expect a day or two's rest will put you right. Would you like Charlotte to come and sit with you later?"

"I'd like her to come now, please," I begged. "I'm not at all sleepy. I'll be very quiet and rest all day, I promise you."

Charlotte brought her sewing in beside me, and with one excuse or another I kept her with me all day. I needed her companionship; I needed her presence to protect me from Rodger.

"It's Janetta's birthday next week; you must be quite better for her party," Charlotte chattered gaily on. "Guess what I am giving her."

I shook my head. "I've no idea," I said.

"I'll fetch it and show you," she cried, and ran out of the room. She was back in a moment bringing with her a small wooden box, a musical box which played a tinkling little tune when the lid was opened. She wound it up and played it to me.

"Oh, how Janetta will love it!" I exclaimed.

"Have you got a present for her or would you like to share the musical box with me?" asked Charlotte. "It's really an old one of mine, but I don't want it anymore so let's share it."

"Oh thank you, you *are* kind, Charlotte," I cried. I really could not afford to buy Janetta a present on my own.

"Will Rodger be at Janetta's party?" I asked.

"Good heavens, no!" cried Charlotte. "Rodger never goes to parties! He avoids other people."

I sighed with relief and began at once to look forward to it.

I was allowed to get up the next day, as I felt so much better, but my spirits were still low, and I was full of fears.

Jocelyn who had called several times to ask after me

was allowed to see me, and when I begged Mrs. Graham very hard she let me walk with him in the garden for a short time. As soon as we were out of sight of the house, he drew me into his arms and began to kiss every inch of my face.

"What happened to you, sweetheart?" he asked. "Why were you out alone in the storm?"

I could not look him in the eye but kept my head lowered as I repeated the lie I had told Catha.

"But where were the Graham boys; why didn't one of them go?" he asked.

"Angus and James were in the gun room doing something to their fishing rods, and Rodger . . . busy with his own affairs," I mumbled. "It was nothing much anyway, and I'm all right now, there's no need to make a fuss."

But my voice trembled, a great sob rose in my throat, and I clung to him as if I were drowning. I longed with all my heart to tell him of the night's happenings, to pour out the whole story to him, but I felt that I must not involve him; it was too dangerous. I did not doubt that Rodger had the power to harm him, and I wanted to protect Jocelyn in every way I could.

He kept his arm round me but his face was troubled and I could see that he did not quite believe me; he knew I was hiding something from him. I wondered what he suspected.

"There's something going on I don't understand," he complained. "Is it Rodger? Has he been bothering you, frightening you?"

"Of course not," I lied, "he is too much occupied with his own affairs to have time for me."

"I'm not so sure," said Jocelyn thoughtfully, "he's a strange fellow, odd and not a bit like the rest of the family. I don't trust him, and I don't like the way he watches you—like a cat with a bird. He is up to no good. You must be on your guard with him, and let me know at once if he becomes a nuisance to you."

"Oh, I'll just keep out of his way," I said to pacify him. "Angus and James are usually about, and Charlotte is nearly always with me."

"Be careful, all the same," Jocelyn advised me, "and try to spend more time with us at Tallows. The Grahams won't mind, I am sure."

"Of course I'll come as often as I can, you know how I love to be with you," I answered, "all of you." He had no idea how much the security and sunshine of Tallows meant to me, how much I counted on it to banish the gloom that Rodger cast me into.

CHAPTER FIVE

As the day of Janetta's birthday party approached, I began to worry about what to wear. I longed for a new frock. I wanted to look my best. I wanted Jocelyn to be proud of me, but everyone knew my few dresses and I was sure they must think them dowdy. Charlotte solved the problem for me by suggesting that I borrow one of hers.

"It's made of the loveliest deep green silk with lace at the neck and wrists," she said, "but Mamma thinks it is a little too old for me, and I have not worn it yet. Do come and try it on, Millie; it will suit you I am sure."

It fitted as if it had been made for me—Charlotte was

big for her age and I small, and I felt that for once I would be as well-dressed as the Grahams or the Parsons.

On the evening of the party I was ready before the others so I decided to go ahead of them to see if I could give Mrs. Parsons any last-minute help. Also I hoped to have a few moments alone with Jocelyn before the others arrived.

I slipped out of the side door of the house, conscious of looking my best, and hurried across the backyard toward the drive. I was excited and delightedly looking forward to the party, and to an evening spent with Jocelyn and his family in their home. But as I passed the old wash house Rodger stepped from the doorway and barred my path. I halted, and all the fears and anxieties I had banished for the evening rushed back into my mind.

"What . . . what do you want?" I faltered.

Rodger smiled slowly, the sly false smile I hated.

"I already have what I want," he replied softly. "Haven't I, my dear, though I see you have discarded my ring—a pity, but no matter, you are bound to me in other indissoluble ways. How charming you look tonight, dear Millie, radiant, glowing, but not for me—for Jocelyn Parsons?"

He was playful, teasing, but like a tiger with its prey, his claws were ready. Suddenly he put his hands on my shoulders and loooked deep into my eyes as if he could read my most hidden thoughts.

"It's no use, Millie," he whispered, "you cannot escape me, *ever*. You had better give Jocelyn up now, before it is too late for him."

"How dare you threaten me, or him," I blustered, deep forces of hatred in me rising with a power I had only sensed was there. "Even if there were no Jocelyn I would still loathe and despise you! Let me pass at once or I shall scream."

He stood aside immediately, his smile faded, and in a rage first, and finally in misery, I fled down the drive to the road.

I felt he had ruined my evening. My eager anticipations were gone, but at least I would be safe from him for a few hours in Jocelyn's home.

Tallows was ablaze with light, and as I hurried toward the house it seemed to hold out welcoming arms to me. I opened the front door and stepped into the hall, and Mrs. Parsons met me at the foot of the stairs.

"Why Millie dear, something has upset you badly," she remarked in her kindest tone." Come up to my room till you recover your composure. You are quite pale."

She put her arm around me and led me up the stairs to her bedroom where I sat down on her bed.

"You have not been quite yourself since the drenching you got on the night of the storm," she said. "You must not overtire yourself this evening, though we are all delighted that you are well enough to come to Janetta's party. Now rest for a little while, and when you feel quite better I will take you down to Jocelyn. I know he is waiting for you."

She left me for a few moments, and I slipped off my wrap and lay down on the bed. She was back very soon, smiling down at me, and I rose to my feet. "What a beautiful dress!" she exclaimed. "The colouring is just right for you. You look charming and most elegant, my dear. Look—I have something here I want to give you, a little keepsake." From its box in her hand she took a brooch in the shape of a golden rose and pinned it onto my dress. "There," she said, "the picture is complete."

"Oh thank you, thank you!" I exclaimed, my even temper restored and my spirits soaring. "Charlotte has lent me this dress for the party, and now you have given me this beautiful brooch—oh, you are all too good to me!"

Mrs. Parsons kissed me gently. "We love you, Millie," she said, "you know that. Ah, now I see that you are better," she continued, "the sparkle is back in your eyes again!"

"I am perfectly all right now," I said, "in fact, I feel wonderful, and so happy. Shall we go down?"

She took my arm and we went down the stairs together. Dear Mrs. Parsons, how fond I was of her; she had admired and complimented me just when I most needed reassurance, she had given me back most of the peace that my meeting with Rodger had destroyed.

There was only time for a few minutes with Jocelyn before the others arrived, and he did not notice any traces of my distress. In the safety and affection of Jocelyn's family and home I was able to give myself up to the enjoyment of the party, and to make my contribution to its gaiety.

Little Janetta was enchanted with her presents, and the musical box was a great success. After supper, when the birthday cake had been cut, we all went into one of the barns which had been cleared for dancing. Mr. Parsons brought out his fiddle and I was initiated into the mysteries of the Scottish reels. I am afraid I did not do very well. I was much more at ease waltzing in Jocelyn's arms, but I enjoyed the fun and my mistakes made everyone laugh.

Angus danced with the doctor's daughter, and James seemed delighted with one of the Robertson girls—another Edinburgh family who came summer after summer to Karasay. Dear James, I was glad to see him happy. I knew he had a fondness for me I could only partially return because of Jocelyn. Charlotte danced with her Robert, her eyes sparkling with pleasure. It was a very gay and informal and happy affair, for they were all friends, and everyone knew everyone present. I was the only stranger but I did not feel one. Janetta's party was an annual event, a sort of highlight of the holiday to which all the Graham group of friends looked forward, and which everyone remembered with pleasure when the holiday was over.

But for me it was an unforgettable night for a different reason. When Jocelyn walked back with me to the Graham's house after the party, he took me through the little wood by the back path that led into the garden, and there he asked me to marry him—"not for a year or two, not till we are both a little older, but at least let us become engaged, promised to one another, my darling," he said. I felt breathless with joy although I had been half-expecting his proposal, and when he drew me into his arms and held me closely I thought my heart would burst with happiness. But I did not know how to answer him, although I loved him deeply and with absolute certainty. I did not dare to commit myself. I thought of Rodger's threats, and since I believed implicitly in his power to damage, to destroy, I felt I had to protect Jocelyn at all costs; I had to play for time.

"I must think it over," I whispered. "Let me talk to my mother before I give you my answer. I must be quite sure before I promise." I wished he knew what it cost me to say this, it was the only way I could think of to safeguard him.

Jocelyn looked at me in astonishment, his face in the moonlight was hurt and bewildered, and no wonder. "I thought you loved me," he murmured.

"I do! Oh I do," I cried. The anguish in my voice must have reached him, for quietly he put his arm round my shoulders and led me on along the path.

"I'll wait," he said gently, "if that's what you want, darling Millie, I'll wait for a while, before I ask you again."

I loved him more than ever for his kindness.

We strolled past the bank where I had found the entrance to Rodger's den on that fatal night, and were nearing the edge of the trees when I saw a movement in the undergrowth. I stopped, startled, and clutched Jocelyn.

"Look!" I exclaimed pointing to the place. "What's that?"

Jocelyn peered between the trees but I was the first to see it, etched dark against the moonlight—"It's a fox!" I cried.

"So it is," Jocelyn agreed, "a big one too, but there's

nothing to be frightened of, perhaps it has a den somewhere in there, though that would be strange so near the
house."

I stood staring at the creature, puzzled and uneasy. It
seemed to be watching us, entirely unafraid, watching us
as intently as a human being would. I shivered and was
reminded of Rodger, of his dark pointed face, of the animal viciousness I had seen in it—there was some connection between it and Rodger, a link that eluded me—when
I looked again the fox was gone.

CHAPTER SIX

I WOKE NEXT MORNING FEELING AS IF I HAD NOT SLEPT AT all. My thoughts were confused, my emotions in a turmoil. I was wildly happy that Jocelyn had asked me to marry him, but distressed that I had not dared to say yes at once. I hated asking him to wait for my answer, and I longed to tell him the whole story, if only I weren't so frightened of Rodger, if only I could doubt his power to harm us. All I could do was to wait, to be as watchful as Rodger, to give Jocelyn my protection.

There was a lot of clearing up to be done after the party, and Charlotte and I went over to Tallows to help Mrs. Parsons, and stayed for lunch. Later in the afternoon they were all coming to tea with the Grahams, so I agreed to meet Jocelyn in the garden just before four, near the summer-house. I made my way back to Karasay House with Charlotte and went up to my room to have a little rest and to change my frock for tea.

I must have dropped off to sleep for when I woke it was almost four o'clock and I had to dress very quickly and hurry to the summer-house; I did not want to be late for Jocelyn.

As I ran across the garden I heard angry voices coming from the path behind the summer-house, disrupting the peace of the drowsy afternoon. I soon saw it was Rodger and Jocelyn, facing one another across the path, each ready to spring at the other.

"Millie belongs to me I tell you," Rodger's voice was bitter and angry, "so be warned and keep off the ground."

"I'm damned if I will," Jocelyn shouted back. "We love one another! What right have you to interfere?"

"I tell you she's mine," Rodger retorted. "I'll never let her go, and if you try to steal her from me you'll be sorry you ever crossed my path."

Jocelyn sprang at him, his eyes blazing, but I rushed and held on to his arm.

"Stop fighting over me," I shouted. "I belong to no one but myself. As for you," I turned to Rodger, "if you harm a hair of Jocelyn's head I'll—" I had meant to say, "I'll go straight to your father," but the words that came out were, "I'll kill you!"

"What a little tiger cat! I believe you mean it," said

Rodger only half amused, but Jocelyn was still choking with rage and I had a hard time trying to drag him away with me towards the house. At last he calmed down a bit though he was still very angry.

"Rodger's mad!" he exploded. "How dare he interfere between us."

"He's dangerous," I insisted. "We must be patient and careful as long as we are on Karasay. Once we leave here and are back in London it will be different. Here, I do assure you, he can harm us."

"What can he do to us?" Jocelyn asked impatiently. "Surely the best way to settle him once and for all is to announce our engagement, then everything will fall into place." ·

"You promised me to wait a little," I reminded him. "Till I have seen my mother, till we are back in London. Surely it's not much to ask, when we have all the time in the world ahead of us."

I believed then that we had.

"I hate your even being under the same roof as Rodger," said Jocelyn. "I wish I could carry you off to live with us at Tallows."

"There is nowhere I'd rather be; you know that," I retorted, "but I cannot offend the Grahams. They have been so good to me, and I am very fond of all of them—except Rodger."

I wondered whether they'd ever invite me to Karasay again? If they did, would I accept in spite of Rodger? I wanted to keep in touch with them, they had become important to my happiness. Perhaps they'd ask me to visit them in Edinburgh; perhaps away from Karasay, Rodger would be different.

There were only two weeks of the holiday left before we all scattered, and as the fine weather held we did not waste our time. Parties of Grahams and Parsons and Robertsons set off every day on some expedition, to explore one of the smaller islands or to visit the main one. There were picnics on the granite cliffs where thousands of sea birds nested and the huge waves tumbled in from the Atlantic; walks to some of the earliest settlements in the land, homes of the stone-age men, four thousand years old. We bathed in the little sheltered bays where the seals played, calling to one another. We watched the fishing boats coming in with their haul, and the fishermen gutting and packing the fish in wooden boxes. And in the evenings we gathered in one of the houses and danced or played cards, or sang round the piano or just sat and talked. It was a simple kindly good way of life. I wished it could go on forever, only Rodger had no place in its pattern. I was surprised that he had made no effort to single me out since the night of the party, had not tried to show his power over me, his frightening possessiveness. I felt he was waiting, watching me constantly, waiting for something to happen before he struck at me again.

I wished I knew what he was up to, but it was impossible for me to follow the dark labyrinths of his mind, to guess what he was plotting. I felt helpless and very much afraid.

CHAPTER SEVEN

SUDDENLY, WITH GREAT VIOLENCE, THE GOOD WEATHER broke in a great storm. Gigantic seas crashed against the cliffs, pounding the solid rocks as if they would crush them to sand. The wind tore screaming around the island leaving destruction in its wake, wrenching the roofs off barns and houses, uprooting trees and harassing the animals in the fields with cold driving rain.

We were prisoners on the island, for no boat dared to venture out until the wind dropped.

Most of us stayed indoors, but some of the boys battled their way across the island and came back dripping, elated by the fury of the storm.

Rodger in particular seemed excited by the wildness of

the weather, which evidently appealed to something ele-
mental in his nature. Every day he went out alone early
and came back late, though where he went to and what
he did nobody knew.

"Be careful you aren't caught by one of those huge
waves," his father cautioned him, but Rodger only
smiled in a superior kind of way. I had the ridiculous notion that if any such danger arose he was quite capable of
escaping, windborne on great wings, like a black-backed
gull. His turbulent presence was strong in the house
even when he was out of it, and I was glad to escape
across the road to Tallows, to the safety and shelter of
the Parsons home.

On the third night of the storm when the gong
sounded for dinner, Rodger did not appear.

"Ring the hand bell at the back door, Catha," said Mrs.
Graham. "He may be in the wash house working on
photographs for the next exhibition and may not have
heard the gong."

Catha did as she was told but there was no response, so
James was asked to go and see if he could find him.

He returned wet and dishevelled shaking his head.

"No sign of him there," he said. "Are his oilskins
about?" asked Mr. Graham, and Angus went to the
cloakroom to look.

"No they're not," he reported when he returned. "He
must still be out-of-doors."

"Well, we'll have to begin dinner without him," said
Mrs. Graham. "Come along. I expect he'll turn up presently."

But night came on, the storm continued to rage, and

Rodger did not return. At first the Grahams were not unduly worried. They were used to his solitary habits and long absences; still it was not the kind of night anyone would choose to stay out of the house.

"He's probably sheltering in some cave on the cliffs, or in one of his photographic hideouts on the moors," Charlotte suggested, but Mr. Graham was more sceptical. "I doubt it," he muttered, "even Rodger would hesitate to stay out-of-doors tonight. But he will not listen to anyone, he always thinks he knows best and he's far too reckless. The cliffs are very dangerous in a storm like this, with those enormous waves breaking over them. He shouldn't be out tonight. I don't like it at all."

Angus and James tried to reassure him.

"You know Rodger, he always turns up all right. He'll be back for breakfast when he's hungry," they said. But Mrs. Graham was growing anxious and to reassure her the two boys offered to go out and search for him. "Though goodness knows where to begin," said James.

"I'll come with you, and we'll start with the cliffs nearest the house," said Mr. Graham.

"I wish we had a dog," said James, "one that knows him, although tracks would be quickly obliterated in rain like this." There had never been a dog in the Graham household because of Mrs. Graham's asthma.

As Mrs. Graham, Charlotte and I sat with our sewing, waiting for Mr. Graham and the boys to come home, a terrible thought came into my mind. I found myself wishing that Rodger would not be with them, that he would never come home again! It was a dreadful thing to wish, but knowing Rodger for what he was, deep down inside myself I felt that for everyone's sake it was the best thing that could happen.

After three hours of exhausting search Mr. Graham and the two boys returned—without Rodger.

"If he's not back by morning we'll organize a big search party," said Mr. Graham. "There's nothing more we can do tonight. It's wilder than ever and very dark."

"I bet we'll find him snoring in his bed in the morning," said Angus, but no one was amused.

Rodger was not in his bed in the morning. Although a large search party of Grahams, Parsons, Robertsons, the island policeman and others, scoured the cliffs and moors the whole of the next day as the storm subsided, no trace of him was found. He had simply vanished, disappeared, gone.

Rodger Graham was never seen again, and his body was never found.

I don't know how the thought came to me, but I began to wonder whether Rodger really had been drowned at all, or whether he had met with an accident in his grim rock chamber underground and might even still be alive. I spoke to no one of my suspicion, not even to Jocelyn, but as the days passed I began to feel a sort of certainty that he lay in the old quarry, which I alone knew of.

I was shocked at myself for keeping silent, but I was determined to tell no one. Rodger was better dead. After all it was he himself who had made me swear never under any circumstance, no matter what happened, to tell any living person of the existence of the rock chamber, nor what I had seen there. Ironically the promise had turned against himself, and I swore once again never never to break it. Yet, at the same time, I knew that I must carry the secret burden of my knowledge for the rest of my life and already that burden had become heavy. It filled me with heaviness and despair. I turned the inside of my wrist to the light and ran a finger along the scar that Rodger had made—more like a brand really or a secret mark, for the cut had not healed in a straight line but was twisted and warped. I shuddered as I touched it for it brought Rodger vividly to life before me, as clearly as if he were really there and I heard again the triumph in his voice as he proclaimed, "You're *mine*, Millie . . . forever." I had the despairing feeling that even if Rodger was dead and could no longer harm Jocelyn, his power over me was in no way diminished; he would overshadow me as long as I lived.

There was an investigation into his disappearance, of course, but nothing fresh was discovered, and Mr. Graham's theory, which seemed the most likely one, was officially accepted: that Rodger had been swept off the cliffs by a huge wave and his body carried out to sea by the current. It was a terrible end to the holiday, and to spare the feelings of the Graham family there was no publicity about the accident and as quickly as possible the matter was closed.

A few days later the Parsons left for London. I had intended to travel with them, but Charlotte had been badly upset by the tragedy, and when Mrs. Graham begged me to stay on with them for a few days, to keep

Charlotte company, I felt it was the least I could do. I suppose I was still in a state of shock myself, for when Jocelyn came to say goodbye to me I could not respond to him as he expected. He seemed uneasy and suspicious and questioned me in a way I did not at all like.

"I have a strong feeling that you know something about Rodger's disappearance," he said. "Is there something you are hiding from me?" He scanned my face anxiously, pleading for my reassurance, but I could not look him in the eye.

"Why should I know anything?" I blustered. "You hated Rodger as much as I did."

"You haven't answered my question," he replied curtly. "I wish I hadn't heard you threaten him. If you know *anything* about his death for heaven's sake tell me."

"I don't know anything," I muttered sulkily. I was annoyed with him for his hinted accusation.

"I think you are lying, Millie; why can't you trust me and tell me the truth?" he asked.

I could not answer him, and we parted coldly.

With the Parsons gone Karasay House seemed more inimical, than ever, dark with a hostility that dismayed and depressed me. I vowed when we finally left that once safely away I would never again set foot in it as long as I lived.

I had imagined that with Rodger gone and the threat to Jocelyn removed, everything would fall into place and Jocelyn and I would become engaged to be married. I thought that once I was back in London everything would be all right. But that is not how the pattern worked out at all. Even in London Rodger haunted me. Gradually I was forced to realize that what he had said was still true: in some inexplicable way I felt myself irrevocably bound to him; his hold over me seemed as strong as ever. He stood like a wall between Jocelyn and me, keeping us apart.

However hard I tried, I could not convince myself that I was free to marry Jocelyn. I could not rid myself of the spell of Rodger's dominance, and there was nothing I could do about it.

I decided at last to write to Jocelyn explaining to him that I was sorry, I had made a mistake, I did not love him enough to marry him and I did not wish to see him again.

It was a bitter letter and cruel but it seemed the only way of finishing all that was between us. No one will ever know what it cost me to write it, loving him as I did.

Jocelyn Parsons and I never met again, and soon after I sent my letter I heard that he had gone to settle in Australia. Later, the rest of the family went to live in Scotland, in Edinburgh.

My friendship with the Grahams continued, and later James and I were married, much to the delight of my mother and I hope of Mrs. Graham. We have a daughter whom we call Alison. James is a good husband, kind and loving and safe; we are happy together and I have grown very fond of him—but he is not Jocelyn. No one could ever take his place and my love for him will not die.

I have kept my promise to Rodger; his secret is safe with me.

No one has ever persuaded me to return to Karasay House, although the Graham families still congregate there every summer.

My stay on Karasay was the turning point in my life. There I stepped out of childhood into maturity. Surely a part of me must linger in the house where so much happened to me that fateful summer, where caught up in the tangle of my developing emotions I first met evil face to face, where I experienced deeply for the first time love, hate and fear. Does the presence of Rodger still cast its shadow over the house? Will the struggle between us vibrate through its rooms for ever? And who will win in the end? I cannot tell—our story is not yet finished, the pattern not yet completed.

PART II

TOMORROW: ROMILLY

CHAPTER EIGHT

GRAN WAS WAITING FOR ME AT THE TINY AIRPORT, AND AS I walked towards her my heart soared with happiness. It was the farthest north I had ever been. The light had a clear lucid quality, the air a purity as of a newborn land.

"How thin you are, darling!" Gran exclaimed as the airport bus took us swiftly along the road between the hills now purple with heather. It was sunny and warm, a golden September day, and when we arrived at the quay and packed onto the little boat that was to take us to Karasay, the sea rolled smoothly without a breaking wave.

"What's Cousin Derwent like?" I asked Gran.

"He's a bachelor as you know and a very nice fellow; you'll like him, though he can be tetchy when his war wound is bothering him. I haven't seen a great deal of him since we were young and all used to come up to Karasay in the summer. It's difficult to keep in touch when we live so far apart."

"Is his home on Karasay? Does he live there all the year round?"

"Yes, but he has a small flat in Edinburgh as well," Gran replied. "It's usually lent to one of the family. He's very well looked after on Karasay; Polly and Greenie have been with him for years—they're locals of course."

"What is his war wound?" I asked.

"It's a wound in his back from the second war that gives him trouble," said Gran. "He has to come south to Edinburgh for treatment."

It took us an hour to cross the sound and to reach the little sheltered harbour of Karasay. It was a smaller island than I had expected, its green and gold fields sloping gently to the sea in dappled patchwork. I was later to discover it had a darker side, sinister as the great rugged cliffs at its back which the Atlantic seas buffeted and lashed in a continous rage.

Screaming gulls announced our arrival, and the people who had come to meet friends off the boat began to wave.

"There he is! There's Cousin Derwent," cried Gran, pointing to a lean bearded man in brown tweeds and a fishing hat, who was waiting on the quay.

My mental picture of a querulous old man rather set in

semi-invalid ways could not have been more wrong.

"Welcome to Karasay, Cousin Romilly," he called, standing at the bottom of the gangway to help us off. "I'm delighted to make the acquaintance of Alison's favourite granddaughter."

"Thank you, Cousin Derwent," I answered. "It's lovely to be here." Then not to be outdone in teasing I

added with a giggle, "You're not as Gran described you!"

"Oh ho! And what was that? I can see you are very like your grandmother," he said laughing. "Come away now, give me your bits and pieces; the car's quite close. Is there a bigger case somewhere?"

"Yes there is; the one with the red stripe around it," I cried, pointing to where the baggage was being thrown from the boat and caught by a young man on the quay.

"Bring it along, Andra, when you can spare a minute," Cousin Derwent called to the young man. "Romilly Williams on the label."

"Aye, I'll bring it, Mr. Graham," Andra replied. He followed us almost at once, put the case into the boot, nodded to Gran and Cousin Derwent and winked at me, then went back to his work. In a few minutes Cousin Derwent's old Morris was chugging up the hill from the village.

Karasay House was much as I had expected it to be and I picked it out easily as we drove toward it, recognizing it from Gran's old photographs. What I had *not* expected was the strange and very strong feeling that I had been there before.

As we turned in at the gate, the house wore a sullen look, scarcely welcoming, and great rooks like black sentinels crouched on the posts of the rusty wire fence that divided the garden from the fields in front of the house.

A woman in a flowered pinafore stood waiting for us on the front doorstep.

"There's Polly," remarked Cousin Derwent, tooting

the horn. "Greenie won't be far behind her." And even as he spoke a second flowered figure appeared.

They swooped on the car like a pair of doves, cooing and fluttering, helping us out, and as soon as I had been introduced they collected my belongings and firmly ushered me into the house. I glanced back and saw Cousin Derwent take Gran by the arm and share some little joke with her before they followed us.

I was conducted upstairs by Polly while Greenie went off to the kitchen muttering about her scones.

"We've put you in this room because it's nice and sunny and faces on to the garden," said Polly, throwing open a bedroom door. "The bathroom is opposite and your Grannie's room next to you. On your other side there's a spare room, empty just now. You'll ask for anything you want, won't you? Greenie and me are awfu' glad to have a young one about the house again." She beamed up at me—I was at least half a head taller than she—and her blue eyes twinkled with pleasure. "*Awfu'* glad," she repeated. "Now come down for tea when you're ready," she said, leaving me.

I closed the door, threw my jacket onto the bed and looked around me. It was a nice little room—walls, woodwork and furniture all painted white. The bed cover and curtains were striped blue and green and there was a large blue rug on the polished floor. On the dressing table stood a vase of roses, and there was a cupboard with shelves for my clothes, a chair or two, and a bed table with a reading lamp. Over the head of the bed hung an old fashioned text— "Thou God see-est me." There was a pleasant atmosphere in the room that had nothing to do with the afternoon sun streaming through its window. It had a repose, a quietness all its own. I sensed it on that first day and the feeling grew the longer I stayed in the house: a sense of being cherished, protected.

Gran called, "Tea's ready, darling," and I shook myself out of my dreaming, ran a comb through my hair, and dashed into the bathroom for a wash.

Cousin Derwent was waiting for me at the foot of the stairs. "Come along, Cousin Romilly," he said. "I hope you're as hungry as I am and can eat a decent tea?"

"I'll do my best," I assured him.

Gran was seated at an oval table, waiting to pour out the tea, in a biggish room with French windows opening onto the garden. This much I had time to see before my attention was concentrated on the wonderful variety of homemade breads, jams, scones, biscuits, shortbread, and three kinds of cake—the most sumptuous tea I had ever seen; even Wales couldn't beat it.

"Tuck in," commanded Cousin Derwent, and with a sigh of pure pleasure, I did.

After a few slices of bread and the first three or four scones had gone down, I paused to have a look around the room.

"I didn't know how starved I was!" I exclaimed apologetically.

Gran smiled encouragement. "I told you you are too thin," she said.

"Don't stop now," begged Cousin Derwent. "I like a lassie who eats a decent tea. In any case those round at the back will not approve unless the plates go out empty."

"He means Polly and Greenie, of course, in the kitchen," Gran explained. "He has to have his little joke at their expense."

I giggled and attacked the plate of shortbread.

At last tea came to an end. I could not have swallowed another mouthful—and I went upstairs to unpack.

Gran offered to help me but I could see she was tired. "Don't bother," I said, "it won't take me more than a few minutes."

"We'll have a look round the garden when you're ready, Cousin Romilly, before the sun goes down," Cousin Derwent suggested.

I ran upstairs, unlocked my case, and in no time my clothes were sorted out and everything neatly stowed in the cupboard.

Cousin Derwent and I went out together, leaving Gran in a comfortable chair in the drawing room. I knew she was longing to have a little snooze.

He led me across the lawn fringed with flower beds to a little summer-house which looked very dilapidated, really scarcely safe to sit in. Behind it was a small neat vegetable garden and from there we followed a path through a copse tangled with brambles and undergrowth and came out on the drive close to the house again, at a group of outhouses and sheds. They were all in a state of disrepair; in fact the roof of one had fallen in.

"Can't afford to keep the place up any more," said Cousin Derwent apologetically. "Very different when

Alison and I were young, I can tell you."

"Alison?" I queried. "Oh Gran, of course. Well, I like a wild garden, not too formal but tidy, you know what I mean."

When we came to the front of the house I noticed how grass-grown the drive was, and how the field needed scything. It all had a neglected look; perhaps Cousin Derwent was short of money.

"How long has this house been your home?" I asked him.

"It was our *holiday* home when we were children and lived in Edinburgh," he said. "Then when my father, Angus Graham, retired because of ill health, he came and settled here."

"And you?" I persisted.

"I took over the house when my father died. The war put an end to my career. I had to spend a long time in hospital, but they've done wonders."

"Oh, yes, Gran said you'd been badly damaged in the war. Were you in the army?"

Cousin Derwent nodded, "Yes, the Intelligence Corps; I wasn't in the fighting. The injury to my back was just bad luck; my Jeep trod on a mine in the desert. I still have a bit of trouble now and then and it needs treatment in Edinburgh. I have a hidey-hole there—sometimes I have to escape from my devoted keepers, you know."

His eyes twinkled with mischief; he was speaking of Polly and Greenie, and I understood just what he meant. They could be overwhelming, smothering, if he let them.

"It's a pity you were not able to come earlier," he continued as we strolled toward the front door. "There have been relays of young Grahams all through the summer staying in the house, and Parsons at Tallows, just as in the old days, the same recurring pattern. You'd have had some good company and got to know some of your Edinburgh cousins; now, you'll just have to put up with two old people."

"Gran's special; I never think of her as old, and I think you are too—special, I mean," I said, smiling at him, "but I'm sorry about my cousins. That's the worst of living in Pembrokeshire; it's so far away—though I love its every little field and bay, its changing colours, each crown of rocks on the moors, every headland and *cwm*,—glen I mean—oh, *everything*, it's home."

"I know," Cousin Derwent nodded understandingly, "it's what I feel about Karasay." I had a sudden unexpected twinge of homesickness for our house, and Jeanie, for the little bay below the house, and the valley that ran down to it where the finest mare's-tails in the whole of Pembrokeshire were reputed to grow.

The sitting room was empty when we got in, but a fire of logs and peat was burning in the grate, and I sniffed the smoke appreciatively. It was rather a faded room. The curtains and rugs had a tired look, and some of the chair covers were beginning to fray. It was old-fashioned too, and I doubted if it had really changed much since my great-grandmother's time.

I noticed several rather good watercolours signed by Cousin Derwent, a few beautiful pieces of china, plenty of books, a television set, a radio, and a really magnificent grand piano.

There should have been a mellowness, a feeling of well-being, the sense of an established order, but in spite of its beauty, the room had a chill, an uneasy air, even a certain hostility, which the cheerful fire did nothing to dispel.

CHAPTER NINE

I CHANGED INTO MY NEW COTTON FROCK, LONG, ALMOST
to the ground, of an apricot colour sprigged with white
flower heads, and I was just tucking my hair under an
Alice band when the notes of a Chopin polonaise, rous-
ingly played, came sharply up to me—Gran no doubt.

But when I hurried downstairs I found not Gran but
Cousin Derwent seated at the piano. He stopped as I entered but, "Go on!" I cried, "please go on, it's marvell-
ously exciting. I had no idea that you were a pianist;
Gran never told me. You are full of surprises."

He went on playing. "Surely it's more fun to discover
for oneself than to be told," he suggested. "I like a bit of

mystery myself, Cousin Romilly, and I agree with you, there is magic in Chopin. Ah—here is Alison." He rose as Gran came in and I turned to her impulsively. "He plays very well, as well as you do!" I cried. "You must have a lot in common."

"Oh we do, we play duets together in the evenings," said Gran laughing. "We exhaust one another with variations."

Cousin Derwent brought her a glass of sherry but I refused my permitted half—it always gave me the hiccups.

"What a pretty frock, darling, it's new isn't it—just right for you. Did you make it?" asked Gran, fingering the skirt approvingly. "It makes you look suddenly grown-up and unfamiliar—and the resemblance to your namesake is quite startling. Don't you agree, Derwent?"

No compliment could have pleased me more, and I was glad that she liked my dress.

"Sarah helped me to make it when she was home in August. She has become very good at dress-making," I explained, "although she goes in for rather weird clothes herself, I think,—beady and bitty, nothing matching, no final pattern."

"And you like a pattern, Cousin Romilly?"

"Yes I certainly do; I like a finish, a completeness," I said emphatically.

"Dinner is ready, sir," said Polly at the door, and we all went into the dining room.

There was fresh salmon, potatoes and salad from the garden, followed by peeled fresh peaches and cream.

"Delicious," I sighed when the last peach slid down

my throat, and Polly retreated satisfied that I was not being starved.

"Home produce," boasted Cousin Derwent. "I might show you where to find them—grown in the greenhouse, of course."

I sound shockingly greedy, but I don't think I am really; it was only that faced with all those super things to eat I suddenly found I had acquired an appetite. Perhaps it was the Karasay air.

Polly and I joked together about putting on weight as I helped her clear the table before I joined the others in the sitting room.

"What would you like to do, Cousin Romilly?" asked Cousin Derwent. "Is there anything on TV you'd like to see—it's not always very reliable but we'll do our best," and he looked across at Gran and smiled. I suspected that they were simply itching to be left together at the piano, and in any case I wanted to explore a bit on my own before it got too dark. I crossed to the open window and sniffed the scented dusk—the rich earthy enticing smell of autumn. "I think I'll go out for a while," I told them. "I want to have a look around."

"Well, don't go too far, and take a cardigan with you," Gran advised.

"I shan't be long. See you later," I replied, and went to fetch a woolly.

The piano was going steadily when I came downstairs, and I couldn't resist pushing the door slightly open and glancing in. They sat at the piano, their two pairs of hands playing most cunningly together, oblivious to everything except themselves and the rhythm of their music. How sweet they looked.

"That might be a splendid idea; they could be very happy together," I thought, as I slipped out and along the passage to a side door that opened onto the yard at the back of the house.

I wandered round the garden for a little while before walking down the drive, scaring the sentinel rooks by flapping my arms at them, and out onto the road.

It was very still. The sky to the west was gently flushed and the first stars had appeared. Curlews were calling from the moor behind me reminding me of home, and as I sauntered down the road towards the village, a chill little breeze off the sea made me pull my cardigan closer around my shoulders.

Just below Cousin Derwent's house on the opposite side of the road I passed a farmhouse with the name "Tallows" on its gate, but it gave no sign of life. Further down the road I came on various cottages dotted down the sides of the descending hill, each with its plume of smoke feathering in the breeze. Then round a bend below me lay the snug little harbour, its grey stone houses nestling round it in a tight design, their windows beginning to twinkle through the dusk as the lights went on.

I stood on the grass verge for several minutes absorbing the compact scene in all its beauty while the wind swept through my hair, till suddenly I felt chilly and turned to walk back up the hill again. As I approached the house called Tallows I noticed a soft glow of light coming from the windows. "Odd," I thought, "there must be someone there after all in spite of its deserted look."

I stepped briskly along Cousin Derwent's drive determined not to be daunted by the sullenness of the house with its circle of brooding birds. To avoid the front, I decided to go in by the side door in the yard. But there, curiosity overcame me and I stopped to peer into the different outhouses. First there was the old stable now used as a garage, then a crumbling building full of neatly arranged gardening tools, another one held a workbench and a stack of firewood, and the last, when I peeped into it, was obviously an old wash house. Its cobwebs and dust and holes in the roof proclaimed it to be a ruin. As I stepped close, I became aware of an intense coldness, which seemed to rise from the stone floor and walls, a paralyzing icy coldness that numbed my limbs and threatened to envelop me.

I picked up my skirts and turned and fled across the yard to the side door of the house, opened it and stepped inside—then I looked back. A boy stood there, a young man, on the threshold of the wash house. It was not light enough to see his features, and in the dusk I could not even be certain that he was real; it could have been a shadow, for when I looked again, he was gone.

The door of the kitchen was open as I entered the house, and Polly heard me and came into the passage to investigate. The piano still echoed from the sitting room.

"We've just made a cup of tea; come in and have one with Greenie and me, won't you?" said Polly, and I didn't have to be persuaded. They pulled an old chair

with a high straw back nearer the fire for me. The front
of the stove was down and a lovely warm glow came
through the bars.

"Is this an Orkney chair?" I asked, running my fingers
along its wooden arms.

"That's right," said Greenie, "worth quite a bit of
money now I'm told."

Polly poured out a cup of tea, and Greenie passed me a
plate of gingerbread.

"I went for a little walk," I explained, "down the hill
toward the village. That's a nice farmhouse down the
road from here—Tallows they call it."

"It belongs to the Parsons," said Polly. "There have
been relays of them up here all the summer, some of
them your age."

"Oh yes, I know about the Parsons," I said. "They've
been coming to Karasay for ages, haven't they?" I
thought of the old photograph album in Gran's house in
London.

"Grahams and Parsons and Robertsons, generations of
them, though the Robertsons don't come no more," said
Greenie dreamily. "Not so many of the old ones left now,
but the young ones still keep on coming."

"But I thought the Parsons had all gone," I remarked.
"The house looked shut up when I passed it, but on the
way back the windows were lighted, so there is still
someone there."

"*The windows were lighted?*" Greenie repeated in-
credulously, peering intently at me. "Are you *sure?*"

"Quite sure," I replied, "the house can't be empty."

"The house *is* empty," said Greenie emphatically. "The Parsons all left a week ago. They shut the house up for the winter and brought me the key, so I know."

"Then, who—?" I began.

"You've just been imagining," said Greenie crossly, and she jumped up and closed the fire door of the stove as if dismissing me for the night.

I had the feeling she was pretending, trying to put me off asking questions; I was almost sure of it,—Greenie knew quite well what I was talking about.

CHAPTER TEN

THE NEXT MORNING WAS GREY AND SUNLESS AND DIS-
tinctly colder. Cousin Derwent had to visit someone on
the other side of the island and Gran was going with him.
When he asked me if I'd like to come too, I shook my
head. I wanted to have a look at the village, to get the
feel of the place. I intended to do the shopping with
Greenie and try to find out more about Tallows.

It was drizzling as we set off down the hill together,
each carrying a basket, and as we passed the house I had a
close look at it—it certainly was shut up, its shutters all
tightly fastened; yet I *knew* I had seen light glowing
from those windows the night before. It was all very

mysterious. I saw Greenie glance at the house and then at me as if she were sizing me up, but when she spoke all she said was, "You see, all shut up as I said."

"Couldn't someone have broken in?" I suggested.

"No one on this island would dare to," said Greenie promptly.

"Why not?" I asked.

"Well . . . because . . . it wouldn't be right," she finished lamely. "It's as I said, you were just imagining."

I said no more just then, but I was certain that Greenie knew much more than she was prepared to tell me yet.

She steered the conversation into safer channels to stop my asking any more questions.

"One of my old aunties used to live there," she remarked, nodding toward a cottage on the way down the hill, and a little further on, "That's my cousin's house, and yon's my uncle's farm on the moor."

Greenie seemed to be related to half the inhabitants of Karasay.

As we waited our turn at the village store, Greenie exchanged the news of the day with others, and introduced me as Mr. Graham's young cousin from Wales. With one basket almost full we next visited the bakehouse. I positively drooled as the delicious smell of new bread drifted toward us and couldn't resist breaking off a crust from the loaf Greenie bought. Lastly we called at the quay where a fishing boat bobbed up and down on the water, and its catch lay spread out for inspection. Greenie spent a long time taking her pick for our supper, then we stopped for a bit to talk to the fisherman, Rob

Flett, another cousin of Greenie's. He was skipper of the island's lifeboat and the strongest-looking man I'd ever seen.

By that time it was raining quite heavily and we'd be pretty wet by the time we got home.

"Never mind, Polly will have the kettle on and we'll have a cup of tea and maybe a scone or two," said Greenie cheerfully.

As we plodded up the hill, two extraordinary figures came out of a cottage ahead of us and started down towards the village. They wore hats and gloves and old-fashioned macintoshes flapped round their ankles. They even carried an umbrella each.

"Here come the Junipers," whispered Greenie to me, "Miss Juniper and Miss Minnie. We'll have to stop and speak." They walked like ducks in a kind of procession, Miss Juniper in front, Miss Minnie a few steps behind her.

"It's a miserable day, Miss Hobbester," stated the elder Miss Juniper, peering at Greenie under the brim of her hat.

"I see you've got a helper," said Miss Minnie, nodding pleasantly to me.

Greenie introduced me to each of them and they were very affable, though I thought Miss Juniper a formidable old woman, angular and stiff, with pale reptilian eyes, cold as marbles. I felt an instant antipathy. It would be as well not to cross *her* path.

Her sister was very different, smaller, and a bit anxious looking; she gave an appearance of meekness, but there

was a spirited twinkle in her eye. She smiled at me in a conspiratorial way and I knew she wanted to be more friendly, but Miss Juniper hurried her away, and Greenie and I went on up the hill.

"What an extraordinary pair," I remarked. "Are they visitors?"

"Oh no—not islanders, of course, but they live here all right; they came from Glasgow maybe ten years ago," Greenie giggled. "Very genteel indeed," she mimicked wickedly.

"There's not much wrong with Miss Minnie," she continued, "except that she's a little simple, poor thing, but the other one—!" Greenie shrugged and glanced back over her shoulder as if she expected the elder Miss Juniper might have overheard her.

"She gives me the creeps," I confided, "—those queer heavily lidded eyes,—a snake woman! Poor Miss Minnie, no wonder she has an anxious expression."

Greenie darted a quick look at me.

"M-hm, you don't miss much," she said, "and maybe you're right about Miss Juniper; she's a queer one."

By the time we reached the house, we were soaked and it looked as if the rain had set in for the rest of the day. I was glad to take off my wet things in the warm kitchen and to sip the mug of tea Polly had just made.

"I'll finish dusting the sitting room and light the fire," said Polly. "Mr. Derwent and Mrs. Robertson will be glad of it when they get in."

"You'll take your lunch in here with Polly and me?" asked Greenie. "Mr. Derwent and your Grannie should be back soon after."

"Oh yes, please," I said, feeling flattered to have been invited. "Is there anything I can do to help?"

"Yes, you can string the beans for me," said Greenie, dumping a basket of them on the table before me, "while I get on with my pastry."

Each of us worked silently at first, and as Greenie's hands rubbed away at the flour and fat, I was reminded of Jeanie and the kitchen at home.

"How long have you been working in this house?" I asked.

"More than thirty years," said Greenie. "Since I was fifteen, and my mother and grandmother worked here before me."

"And Polly?"

"Polly only came when Mr. Derwent took over the house. Her family belongs to another island, Holmsay, across the bay from here. *We've* always lived on Karasay."

"Then *your* grandmother," I said slowly, thinking it out, "must have been working in the house when my *great*-grandmother came here on a visit to the Grahams —that must have been more than seventy years ago. I'm called after her—she was the Romilly Carpentier who married James Graham."

Greenie chuckled. "You know it all off pat," she said. "I suppose your Grannie has told you. Oh yes," she continued, "I mind how my grandmother, Catha Flett, used to talk about Romilly Carpentier and her visit to Karasay —it was the summer Rodger Graham disappeared."

"He was drowned, wasn't he?" I prompted her, remembering what Gran had told me about him.

"Well, they thought he must have been swept off the cliffs in the storm," said Greenie. "Anyway he vanished and was never seen again."

"How terrible. And no one ever found him—his body I mean?" I asked.

"Never," said Greenie, "never a trace; he was only eighteen years old."

"He would have been a brother of my great-grandfather's," I said. "I wonder what really happened to him? I'm fascinated by the Graham family; it's like a jigsaw you have to piece together. I'd like to find out more about it."

"There are plenty of old photograph albums in the sitting room if you're interested," Greenie told me. "You'll find them in the cupboard at the bottom of the bookcase."

"They're probably much the same as Gran has," I said, "but perhaps they go back further. I'd like to have a look at them." I told Greenie about the game I used to play with the people in the old photos when I was little and stayed with Gran in London. "They were quite real to me then," I said. "I had forgotten how fond I grew of them, the funny old photograph people! I'll go and find the albums as soon as I've finished these beans."

Greenie folded her pastry once more into a neat parcel, dusted the flour off her hands and went out of the kitchen. She came back in a moment bringing a little wooden box, which she put beside me on the table.

"These belonged to my grannie, to Catha," said Greenie, "nothing of value but little things she had when she worked in the house, keepsakes likely. You can have any of them you have a fancy for."

"Oh, thank you, Greenie!" I cried. "I'd love to have a look at them anyway; thank you very much." Soon I finished stringing the beans and went off into the sitting room, where I sat down on the floor near the fire, opened the box and tipped its contents out before me. There was a strange assortment of things, junk mostly but interesting—a carved bone button; a pebble of semi-precious stone, polished and rose-coloured; a scrap of handmade lace; a little finger ring of stone curiously marked; half a locket containing a curl of hair; an embroidered pocket; a faded photograph of Karasay House; a tiny key on a piece of velvet ribbon; a broken string of beads. I examined each of the treasures in turn, and last of all I picked up the little stone ring and held it up towards the firelight, which transformed it to a glorious green colour. I slipped it on to the third finger of my left hand, and it fitted perfectly. I held my hand at arm's length turning it about, admiring the ring, examining the design that was carved round it, then I slipped it to the knuckle to take it off and it wouldn't come—it was stuck; I couldn't get it off! I twisted it, pulled it, wrenched it; I even fetched a piece of soap and lathered my finger till it was slippery, but the ring stayed on.

"My knuckle must have swollen," I told myself. "It's bound to slip off later, as easily as it went on."

I put the rest of the things back in the box and fetched

the albums of old photographs from the cupboard in the bookcase, then curling up on the couch I opened the earliest one. The photos were faded, some of them quite yellow with age, and under each one was written in white ink the names of the people in it, or the place. They were mostly holiday photos, picnic groups, gatherings around a wagonette, or formally arranged family photos taken in the garden or on the steps of a house. Some of them I had seen before in Gran's album, but there were many I had not—older photographs of earlier Grahams. I recognized Karasay House, and Tallows, and one taken of the island from a boat in the harbour. I passed quickly over those pages and came to a photograph that interested me much more, an attractive photograph of a charming young girl in a long dark dress, with demure white collar and cuffs. Underneath it was written "Romilly (Millie) Carpentier at Karasay, Summer 1901." I smiled into the face of my great-grandmother.

CHAPTER ELEVEN

THERE WERE SEVERAL GROUPS ON KARASAY IN WHICH THE first Romilly appeared, and those were the photos I pored over—"The Graham family with Romilly," "Romilly, Charlotte and James," and another "Romilly with Angus, Rodger and James"; then there was one of her standing beside a marvellous-looking young man. "Romilly and Jocelyn Parsons," it said. That was all, only those few photos, then she never appeared again. Further on there were photographs of Gran as a young girl which I'd seen before in her own album in London— Gran at Karasay with her father James, Gran with Cousin Derwent, with her uncles and aunts and cousins,

but never with her mother. There were no photos of
Romilly *Graham* at Karasay. I was disappointed and
soon lost interest in the other Grahams, except Rodger,
whom I found fascinating, partly because of the mystery
about him, partly because of his strangely haunting face.
As I stared at him, concentrated and intent, a kind of
awareness began to stir in me, and my heart started to
thump with excitement. I was transported back into my
childhood world of shadows, back into the game I used
to play in Gran's house when I lived under the spell of
those Victorian ancestors of mine.

The lunch bell brought me abruptly back to the present and I realized I was extremely hungry. All through
lunch Greenie and Polly plied me with questions about
Pembrokeshire and I told them all I could about our
home, about Jeanie, about my brothers and sisters.

"I'm the middle one, you see," I explained. "Like the
cat who walks by himself I go my own way."

"And what way is that?" asked Greenie.

"Well . . . I like to have time to myself to think and
to dream. I don't like being one of a crowd all looking
and acting alike—that's the way Sarah likes to live, especially since she went to London, but I'm different; I like
to be an individual and do my own thing in my own
way."

"Do you mean your drawing?" Polly asked. "Mrs
Robertson was telling us how good you are at it."

"Well, yes, I do mean that partly, it's something I
really care about, but it's more than that, it's the way I
want to live, a special plan for my own life to be made by
me."

Greenie regarded me silently for a moment. "You're something quite special already!" she exclaimed. "It was *you* who saw the windows of Tallows alight when the house was empty and deserted. It takes someone very special to do that."

"So you believed me all the time," I said, laughing. "You *knew* I wasn't imagining it. Tell me about it, please."

"It's an old story now; my grannie told me years ago. She said that when the summer is over and everyone's gone, ghosts of the family come back to Tallows—Parsons of Catha's time, just for a week or two—the Autumn People, she used to call them. She was always happy while they were here."

"And the people of Karasay still believe this. . . . Is that why no one would dare to break into the house?" I asked.

"That's right," said Greenie, "although it's a few years since my grannie died, the superstition persists, the old beliefs still go on here on Karasay, you know."

"I wonder why they come," I asked, "the Autumn People, I mean?"

Greenie smiled. "Because they were happy here, and there was something about keeping some pattern of family tradition alive to hand on to the younger folk; that's what my grannie used to say. But maybe you'll find out for yourself when the right time comes," said Greenie. "I see you're wearing the ring from Catha's box; it fits you very well."

"Where did it come from?" I asked. "Who did it belong to?"

"I haven't a notion," said Greenie, taking my hand to look more closely, "but it's kind of curious, unusual, isn't it?"

"*Most* unusual," I replied, but I did not tell her the most curious thing about it, that it refused to come off my finger!

When lunch was over I went back into the sitting room and had another try at removing the ring, but it was no use, I could not get it off. So I settled myself comfortably with the album on my knee, and lazily turned its pages, letting my mind wander and dream.

Suddenly, eerily, the room was no longer empty. The house echoed with voices, not clear enough to hear what was said but a jumble of voices, snatches of conversation low and soft, sudden tinkles of laughter. Shadows flitted around me misty and vague, indistinguishable, but I knew who they were, I recognized them as the people who had once lived in the house—the photograph people from the old album. I seemed to have developed an extra sense, a higher degree of perception; where before I had lingered on the fringe of the family group, now I had been admitted to its centre, its heart. I twisted the ring on my finger round and round—there *must* be a connection between it and my new awareness. Was it my passport into the magic circle of the house?

I don't know how long I'd have sat there mouselike, my heart fluttering with excitement, waiting for what was to happen, but all in a moment the atmosphere was shattered by the noise of a car driving up to the door. Uncle Derwent and Gran had arrived back.

I sprang up to blow the fire into crackling flame with

an ancient pair of bellows, then out I hurried to help Gran off with her damp coat and bring her in to get warm.

It was evening before I could be alone, and I knew that it was when I was alone that I would make contact with the house again. After dinner when we had watched a travel film on TV and listened to the news, I fetched my drawing block and having curled up on the couch with it I took out my pencil. Gran and Cousin Derwent moved across to the piano and began to play together. I went on drawing and waited expectantly for the sound of the music to fade, to recede, and the voices of the house I had heard earlier to begin. But I was conscious only of the sighing and creaking of the house around me. It remained empty and the shadow people did not come. The rain still poured down dismally in the darkness, and after a while I grew tired of drawing and decided to go to bed.

"Sweet dreams," said Gran, as I kissed her good night. "I'll look in when I come up if your light is still on."

I was outside the sitting room coming into the hall when I first felt the wave of coldness; it followed me up the stairs, and as I approached my bedroom it increased in intensity so that I felt chilled to the bone. I ran the last few steps to my door, wrenched it open and slammed it hard behind me.

The curtains were drawn and Polly had turned on the electric fire and the reading lamp; my room was warm and comforting and cosily reassuring. Soon I was safely in bed, where, soothed by the softness of blanket and pillow, I stopped shivering and relaxed.

Under the bedclothes my fingers found the little stone

ring and began to turn it about, trying once again to get rid of it—but it was useless; the ring was evidently on to stay. Why, I wondered, had I been admitted to the inner circle of the house? What was required of me, and why *me?* I puzzled over the coldness that had caught me on the stairs; was this part of the hostile element that disturbed the rhythm of the house, that disrupted its peace and made the atmosphere uneasy? It had followed me right up to my bedroom door and there it had stopped. It had not entered my room, and for this I was grateful.

By the next morning the rain had cleared and I was wakened by the sunshine streaming into my room. I jumped out of bed and dressed, it was such a marvellous morning I could not stay indoors. I hurried outside, whistling to myself, and began to wander down the hill toward the village. Everything was sparkling and slightly crisp with an early frost, and in the clear rain-washed air the view, spread out like a tapestry before me, was breathtaking: the little stone houses each with its plume of smoke, the neat harbour with its painted boats, the shining sea, and in the distance the blue humps of other islands silhouetted against the vast expanse of the sky—it was magical!

I had nearly reached Miss Juniper's house when I noticed someone coming across the fields toward the road; it was Miss Minnie. Her head was bent and she was deep in thought so that she did not notice me till she stepped off the field path on to the road where I was waiting for her.

"Oh!" she squeaked, like a startled mouse. "Oh! it's

you, what a nice surprise. I've just been up the hill to the rowan tree—look, my feet are soaking. Isn't it a beautiful morning?"

She was wearing bright blue stockings. "Oh, I like those," I cried admiringly.

"My sister doesn't approve," said Miss Minnie, glancing down at them. "I only wear them when I take a bit of time off for a spree on my own," she explained.

In her hand she was carrying a branch of rowan bright with berries.

"Here, you must have a bit," she said, breaking off a good-sized twig and handing it to me. "I always keep a piece in my room; it's safer, you know—it's a protection."

"Protection from what?" I asked, taking the twig in my hand.

"From—ill-wishers," she whispered, and she glanced behind her as if fearing to be overheard.

Then she gave a little giggle excusing herself for a foolish fancy.

"I wish I could ask you to the house," she said, "but my sister does not care for visitors. Never mind, we'll meet again around and about I expect."

She gave my shoulder a little pat and hurried off down the hill to her home.

Amused but puzzled, I walked back up past Tallows, sleeping behind its shutters, to our gate, then up the drive and into the house. I took the rowan twig to my room and stood it in a glass of water on my bedside table.

What had Miss Minnie meant? What ill-wishers? Had she been trying to give me some sort of warning? Perhaps she felt that something threatened me, that I needed protection. Or perhaps as Greenie had said, she was just slightly simple.

Two or three days passed, glorious golden days, while I explored the island and visited other neighbouring ones with Gran and Cousin Derwent.

I was enjoying myself; we all got on so well together and Karasay was so lovely. But Cousin Derwent felt it was dull for me.

"I like being on my own," I assured him. "More exciting things happen when one is alone."

I was thinking of the house, of course; how absorbing I found it, and how I hoped its mysteries would unfold to me more and more if I were patient and waited.

CHAPTER TWELVE

THE FIRST WEEK OF MY HOLIDAY PASSED AND MY PRE-
occupation with the house deepened. I became more
aware of the tension, the unease in the background of the
house—though its present occupants seemed unaffected
by it. I discovered nothing new, but there were moments
when I felt frightened, threatened. There were certain
rooms I tried to avoid because of their hostile vibrations:
particularly the hall and stairs, the bathroom, and the
little spare bedroom beyond mine. But my own room
was safe, a refuge; in there I had a feeling of protection.

One evening when I came in from the garden, I saw
again by the wash house the same shadowy figure I had
seen on the night of my arrival: again an intense coldness

surrounded him; again he vanished before I could see his face. Although he had never appeared to me inside the house, the coldness was often present, spreading through the hall and up the stairs and along the passage outside my door to the room beyond.

Then at the beginning of the second week in the grey light of early morning I woke from a dream with a terrible thirst. I *had* to have a drink of water. I went out into the passage and across it to the bathroom. There I filled a tooth glass with water, which I gulped down, and as I refilled it I felt the coldness behind me, creeping closer, wrapping me around. I turned, and there, standing in the doorway, was the boy I had seen by the wash house. My knees turned to jelly, and I had to grasp the edge of the bath to steady myself. He was not solid flesh and bone like a real person; his outline was blurred more like an impression on the air, and I recognized him for what he was. As I stared at him I grew frightened and then terrified so that I began to shake. I felt my hair begin to stiffen and prickle, for although his face was hidden from me I did not have to see it to feel the horrible impact of evil. Wildly I tried to think of a prayer, some sort of exorcism to say, but the right words would not come. Then suddenly I remembered Jeanie, on the day the thunderstorm had frightened her out of her wits, and the rune she had used flashed into my mind. I shut my eyes and repeated it aloud.

> "This ae nighte, this ae nighte,
>   Every nighte and alle,

> Fire and sleet and candle-lyte,
> And Christe receive thy saule."

When I opened my eyes again the figure in the doorway had vanished, the coldness was gone, I was alone and safe! I knew now what Jeanie had meant by the terrible power of evil. The terror I had felt chilled me to the bone.

I hurried back to my room, jumped into bed, and buried my head under the bedclothes. Thank heaven there was still safety in my room and that comforting sense of being watched over, but I wondered how long it would last. Had the room once been Romilly's; was she my guardian angel? I had left Miss Minnie's twig of rowan by my bedside—not that I really believed in its power but because she had given it to me, and she was sweet. Still one never quite knows how magic will work, and after the fright I had had it was comforting to see it there under my bed light. I lay awake for ages, unable to sleep, and I began to think of Miss Minnie, because of the rowan twig, I suppose. She was the only person outside our household I could call a friend, and I was surprised to find how fond of her I had become. I had seen her almost every day since our first meeting, sometimes twice in a day. She had the most extraordinary way of bobbing up suddenly in unexpected places, almost as if she lay in wait for me. Once when I climbed the hill beyond the house I had found her sitting under the rowan tree, eating an apple and munching a bar of chocolate.

"Jennet's gone to one of her old meetings, so I'm just

taking a little time off to enjoy myself," she explained, "—here, have a bite."

"Thanks! What kind of meeting?" I asked. The elder Miss Juniper did not seem to me to be the kind of person to connect herself with church or village activities or even politics, and I wondered what she was up to.

"Och, just meetings," said Miss Minnie. "Not for the likes of you or me," she added, dropping her voice to a whisper. Suddenly she burst out laughing, jumped up and pulled me to my feet. "Come on," she cried, "let's get to the top and have a look at the sea on the other side of the island."

She was wearing her blue stockings with faded sand shoes, and her wide flowered cotton skirt was too long, but she hitched it up and together we struggled panting to the top of the hill. She ran surprisingly fast for someone of her age and her gaiety was irresistible. I found her funny and intriguing and most endearing.

Another time when I went down to the harbour with my drawing paper and crayons, I'd only been there for a few minutes when Miss Minnie appeared. She produced a packet of biscuits and sat entranced watching me. I began to think of her as a kind of guard dog who liked to keep me under observation. She was quite a character, and although Greenie thought her simple-minded, her wits seemed pretty sharp to me; she was eccentric perhaps and variable, and a bit scared of her formidable sister, but she was courageous too, although she was quite old and fragile looking.

Once when we had met by chance on the other side of

the island and were walking home together, an Alsatian rushed out from a farm, headed straight for us, barking furiously. I don't like Alsatians much and I had nothing to ward him off with if he did attack us, but little Miss Minnie sailed in brandishing her old umbrella and shouting threateningly, and the dog turned tail and fled.

"It's a splendid thing, an umbrella," she remarked. "I like always to carry mine, and you never know when it'll come in useful as a parachute." I roared with laughter and we went hilariously down the hill together.

But once or twice when I had met her she had looked very subdued and timid, and I thought she had been crying. Although she didn't say anything, and I could not ask, I was certain that sister of hers bullied and somehow frightened her.

I went on thinking about Miss Minnie till at last I fell asleep.

That same day, the day I had finally met the ghost boy in the house, I went to the far end of the island with Greenie. It was her day off and she asked me to go with her to her cousin's farm. There I played with four adorable collie pups, and when the time came for us to leave, one of them attached himself devotedly to me.

"Take him back with you if you like and keep him while you're on Karasay," Greenie's cousin suggested. "He's a good little dog, aren't you, Merman? I'm sure he won't be any trouble, and Greenie can bring him home here after you've gone."

I turned eagerly to Greenie. "What will Cousin Derwent have to say about him?" I asked.

"I don't think he'll mind. He's not fond of dogs, but the puppy can live in the kitchen when he's not outside with you, Romilly. I think you should take him."

So I tucked Merman into my anorak and we started on the walk home. He was a dear little dog, well behaved for a puppy only a few months old, and I was delighted to have him. Cousin Derwent had no objection to his making his home in the kitchen, and although I'd have liked to have had him sleeping in my bedroom, Greenie advised me not to.

"Mr. Derwent might object to that," she said, so we tucked him into a box with a piece of old blanket and a hot-water bottle for company, and he was fast asleep in the kitchen before Greenie and Polly went up to bed.

I was thinking of the puppy and planning what I would do with him the next morning as I climbed the stairs to my own room. Wafts of music came up to me from the sitting room where Gran was playing to Cousin Derwent.

Dreamily I opened my door to put on the light—and stopped; the creeping coldness I had learned to dread met me on the threshold and beyond, standing by my bed, waiting for me, was the ghostly boy. In the dusk I could not see his face, but his presence in my room was enough. I was petrified. He took one step toward me and I went half-mad with fright. My room was no longer safe from him, there was nowhere in the house where I could escape from him! I had to get away, outside, anywhere!

I turned and shot down the stairs, across the hall, and out of the door. Along the drive I raced, through the gate and down the road towards the village. It was an instinctive blind unreasoning flight. I did not know where I was going, I only knew that I must get away, out of the house. I ran on, panting and gasping, never even looking back to see if I was being followed. I ran till I came to Tallows, and saw the light shining from its windows; I rushed at the door, turned the handle and burst into the hall. Motherly arms were held out to me and as I threw myself into them sobbing, a gentle voice said soothingly —"Why Millie my dear, whatever is the matter?"

CHAPTER THIRTEEN

Mrs. Parsons led me into the drawing room where Jocelyn and Robert and Janetta in her dressing gown were playing a game of cards with their father.

"This poor child has had a bad fright," she said. "I'm going to make her a hot drink." The three men jumped up and Jocelyn took my hand in his and fussed over me. I was settled into a comfortable chair and ·gently questioned about what had scared me. But I was unable to give any coherent explanation of what had happened; my mind seemed confused. I only knew that there was something I must not tell them about, and presently they stopped asking. I felt safe with these people, Jocelyn's family. I knew myself cherished and loved and accepted as one of themselves. And Jocelyn himself, so gentle and courteous and loving, there was no one like him. I stayed with them till I had quite recovered from my fright.

I would have liked to stay all night with them, but I knew I must go back to the Grahams, back to Karasay House.

"Come to us as often as you can, Millie," Mrs. Parsons said as she bade me goodnight. "We love to have you with us."

"I'll take you back to Karasay House," said Jocelyn, opening the front door for me—but it was too late, the instant I stepped over the threshold there was a change in me. I found myself alone outside and dazed as if I had been dreaming.

I hurried back to bed thinking that I had been sleep-walking, and it was not until I woke next morning and remembered what had happened that the strangeness of the whole evening suddenly hit me—I had *known* the people in Tallows, and they had known me. We had recognized one another; we did not meet as strangers—I had been there before! And they had called me *"Millie."* I thought hard for a moment—Millie was my great-grandmother, the first Romilly . . . they had mistaken me for her. I had stepped back into her time and had taken part in a scene that must have happened when she was a girl. They were a group of shadows from the old photographs—*they* were the Autumn People!

It was not nearly breakfast time, but I was much too excited to wait. I hurried into my clothes and ran downstairs. I had meant to tell Greenie all that had happened, but the moment I saw her solid bulk in the kitchen I changed my mind. I'd tell no one, not yet anyway; the Autumn People were *mine*, and I didn't want to share them with anyone.

"Well, you're up early," Greenie remarked cheerfully. Then looking at me more closely, "What have you been up to?" she asked. "You look like the cat when he has stolen the cream."

"I had a beautiful dream, and it has left me very happy," I told her. It was true, meeting the Autumn People *had* been a kind of dream.

Polly came in then, bringing her dusters to shake out of the back door. "Better put the kettle on," she said, and did so.

When she had gone back to her dusting, I turned again to Greenie.

"Is this house supposed to be haunted?" I asked her. "It's quite old, isn't it? Is there a ghost?"

She looked at me sharply. "There *is* a ghost," she said, "though I've never seen it. Why do you want to know? Have you seen something?"

I nodded. "Yes, the ghost of a boy, a young man. I've never seen his face," I said, "but he's about in the house. I've seen him several times. He frightens me, he's some-how—horrible."

"Och havers!" cried Greenie. "It's only Rodger Graham; he's the ghost that walks this house."

"Rodger Graham?" I repeated stupidly.

"That's right," Greenie replied, "he's the boy who disappeared in my grannie's time and was never found. *He'll* not harm you."

I did not contradict her; I didn't want to talk about him any more. But of one thing I was certain: whatever Greenie might say, Rodger Graham was *not* harmless.

Then Polly came back and began to lay the kitchen table. "Better have some breakfast with us," she said, "and then maybe you'd like to take the puppy out—I've shut him into the greenhouse for the moment, he's making such a noise."

In my agitation I had forgotten all about the little creature. I swallowed a cup of tea and hurried out to the greenhouse where Merman was barking his head off. He went mad with excitement when he saw me and kept tripping over his own feet when I let him out and took him for a good romp.

When he was tired, I picked him up and carried him tucked into my anorak as I strolled down the hill toward Tallows.

I tried the handle of the door but it was locked, the windows were shuttered, the house was again deserted. I thought of the previous night, of the welcome and the warmth and the kindness, of the blessed feeling of safety the Autumn People gave me, and I knew I would visit them again.

On my way back Miss Minnie came across the fields toward me. There were flowers in her hair and she was tripping along the path wearing her blue stockings and singing in a high breathy little voice. I called to her and waved, and she saw me and came hurrying to where I waited on the road.

"You're all right, are you?" she inquired. "Enjoying your visit, are you?"

"Oh yes, thank you," I replied. I felt tempted to tell her about Tallows and my new friends there, guessing how it would delight her, but then I thought it better to keep them secret, my own private magic.

"Well, what's going on?" she asked. "Whose is the puppy?"

"Borrowed from Greenie's cousin," I said. "Isn't he a little darling?"

The puppy licked my face ecstatically, struggling to get free. "I prefer cats myself," said Miss Minnie, "or foxes."

"*Foxes!*" I exclaimed. "Do you know of any?"

"Mhm, there's one I see often, but I cannot get near him," she replied. Then bending toward me she whispered, "*She* was out again last night at one of her meetings—it was full moon, you know."

"Miss Juniper? Your sister, do you mean?" I asked. She nodded.

"They always meet at full moon," she said. "They think I don't know, but I could surprise them if I chose to." She chuckled mischieviously. "Now I'll be off; she'll be wanting her breakfast," and before I could ask her to explain what she meant she was gone.

I wished I could have pinned her down to tell me more about the elder Miss Juniper. I thought of those pale cold eyes, and a shiver ran up my spine. What was she, **a wise woman**? A witch?

Miss Minnie's interest in foxes must have aroused mine and made me more noticing, for several times in the next few days I spotted the fox. Once I even saw him in the garden, in the wild place behind the wash house where the trees grew in a little copse and there was a wild tangle of undergrowth clustered over a rocky bank. It was a dank dark place and felt as if the sun never reached it, a place of cobwebs and spells and unhappy enchantments. As a rule I kept to the other side of the garden but when, one evening, I saw the fox again, it was poised on the far edge of the lawn, almost as if he were waiting for me, and I was so intrigued I decided to follow him. Stealthily I approached him and he did not move till I was quite near, then he turned and unconcernedly trotted off toward the copse and I followed him. He padded along the path under the trees till he came to the bank in its tangle of thicket,—and there he disappeared. He must have a den in the bank, I thought, wishing that I could find it. But it was getting dark, so this was not the moment for exploration, particularly of such an uninviting place. I would have to come and have a good look another time.

For a number of days after I was busily occupied—in the kitchen helping Greenie to make plum jam, and on an all-day expedition with Gran and Cousin Derwent to the main island. The streets of its little town, Portness, were cobbled, its shops still busy with the last of the summer visitors. Gran bought me a Shetland pullover with a lovely Fair Isle pattern, and we had a quick look around the museum with the most obliging caretaker, looking at the cases stuffed with relics of the stone age. A friend of

Cousin Derwent's lent us his car, and we were able to visit some of the lonely bays and inlets and the remnants of stone villages of early people who had lived on the islands two thousand years ago. There were burial chambers too of even earlier peoples, long lines stretching back into prehistoric times; and on the wild headlands looking eastward there were Viking graves. Here was a richness of history that little Karasay did not possess. I had never seen such myriads of sea birds as gathered there on the cliffs, filling the air with their wild crying, which even drowned the thunder of the waves. I liked to think that the birds were there even before the first men claimed the islands for their home.

The next day we went sailing; and then on her day off, Polly and her brother who was a fisherman, took me out in his boat and we caught mackerel and cod and even two or three crabs. I peered down through the clear water to the sandy bottom hoping to spot a sea monster, a giant ray or shark, a dolphin or a mermaid, but I was unlucky.

Every evening when dinner was over I encouraged Gran and Cousin Derwent to start on their music—not that they needed much encouragement, and I slipped away down to Tallows to my friends the Autumn People. I knew they would be waiting for me, anxious to welcome me into their circle. My delight in them was fully returned; I knew I was dear to them. The moment I stepped over the threshold of Tallows the change took place, and I became Millie, Romilly Carpentier, my own great-grandmother. Without the slightest difficulty I crossed the border of time from my world into theirs. Their world of leisure and repose, their pattern of order and grace, appealed to some deep need in me. Its very formality, its unhurried tradition made me feel secure. I stopped thinking out how such a thing was possible; it was enough that I could span the years at will.

And there was another reason for my happiness at Tallows, a new experience for me. I had plunged into Millie's love affair with Jocelyn Parsons. I had never had a boy friend myself, never been in love, and now I found I was deeply involved in Millie's romance. I knew her joys and her griefs, her ecstasy at being in love and being loved by Jocelyn. It was all second-hand I know, but I felt it was all happening to *me*. Some days, though there was always enough to keep me busy, I could hardly wait for evening to come. I felt at home with the Parsons as I had never felt at home anywhere before. I wanted to see them all, to feel a part of their lives, to be with them, especially Jocelyn.

So in spite of the brooding tension in Karasay House, in spite of Rodger's disturbing shadow, my days on the island had become the happiest of my life, because of the Autumn People. To be with them was pure joy.

CHAPTER FOURTEEN

BY NOW MORE THAN HALF MY TIME ON KARASAY WAS gone. I had only ten days left, so I decided to have one of them entirely on my own. It would give me time to see the island on my own and also time to think about the Autumn People in a way that was difficult with others around. I loved to think about them, to wonder about them, to anticipate the evening. I went to find Polly immediately after breakfast to ask her to make me some sandwiches.

"Now you be careful, my bonnie," she cautioned, as I stuffed them and a couple of apples and a box of matches with my drawing tablet into the pocket of my anorak.

I did not take Merman with me. He was still too small to take on a full day's expedition, and I meant to walk right across the moors to the furthest point of the island. It was a perfect morning when I set off, there was sunlight everywhere and I felt I hadn't a care in the world, once I had left the house behind me.

I saw scarcely a person all day, apart from the odd crofter or shepherd in the distance busy about his own affairs. I was alone on the moors with the curlews and peewits, and it was almost as good as being in Pembrokeshire. I ate my lunch of sandwiches in a little dip on the cliff edge, looking across infinite miles of blue sea to the west. I copied some of the curious natural patterns on the slabs of rock on which I sat, and I fell asleep in the sun.

When I started on the walk back, it took me longer than I expected for I lost the track more than once and had to plough through gorse and deep heather. By the time I reached the path down the hill behind the house, I was tired and more than ready for a long cool lemon drink in Greenie's kitchen. But as I approached the gate into the back garden, I stopped. A fox, his front paw poised in the air, stood watching me. I could not be sure whether he was the same one I had seen before or not, but I thought he must be. After a moment he trotted off toward the copse in the garden, and tired as I was I could not resist following him.

As before, near the bottom of the bank behind the house he disappeared. I picked up a stout stick, and began to whack about in the undergrowth hoping to find his den. I got right up close to the rock and had almost given up the search when I found what I was looking for—a large hole—like the entrance to a tunnel. I tore away the tangled creepers which covered it, knelt down, and began to wriggle my way in. After a minute I stopped. It was hard going and I was tired, the place was dank and had a pungent smell, and the fox, if indeed this was his home, might resent my intrusion. I had begun to back out, when I heard, sharp in the stillness, a whimpering, a stifled whining as of some small animal paralyzed with fright. It came from the tunnel ahead of me, stopped, and then was repeated. I knew that I had to go on, to find out what it was and rescue it.

I clenched my teeth, felt for the matches in my pocket, and went on into the tunnel. The whimpering grew louder and suddenly it dawned on me what it might be.

"Merman!" I called, "Merman! Good dog, brave puppy! Where are you?"

I struck a match and crawled out of the tunnel into a sort of room, a chamber quarried out of the rock. Immediately the whining increased into a shrill barking, and as if my voice had released him from a trap, Merman rushed toward me, limping but falling over himself in his relief to see me. I caught him up to me; he was trembling as he licked my face ecstatically, but his hair bristled along his back. He was still obviously terrified and went on whining even in my arms. His damaged paw hung limply but it did not feel broken, probably just bruised, but the match had gone out and I could not examine it.

Still holding the puppy I struck another match and

peered round the room. It was empty: no fox, no living creature except myself and the little dog. Before me I saw a stone table and on it a candle or two. Behind it on some stone shelves in the wall were arranged the skeletons of a dozen small animals: mice, squirrels, a few birds, a weasel or stoat, but all of them grotesquely shaped, twisted, horrible. There was a collection of nasty little images made of clay, and several jars and bottles half-full of substances. On the wall hung the wizened mask of a fox and what was left of the brush, and on the table lay an assortment of rusted knives, nails, a branding iron and some long needles. What chamber of horrors had I stumbled into? The whole place reeked of black magic, of witchcraft. Then I noticed the roof, which was rough and jagged with splinters of stone, and there was a hole where one of them had fallen out and a faint light filtered through.

Then, just before the match went out—I saw it. I gulped with shock and hastily struck another match and lit the candles. I would not be left in the dark in such a horrible place.

Then I forced myself to look again. A human skeleton lay on its back on the floor, its head crushed under the piece of rock that had fallen from the hole in the roof, a few rotted wisps of clothing still clinging to its naked bones. It was the first skeleton I had ever seen.

I clutched Merman close to me, hugging him convulsively till he squealed, and I turned away in horror, burying my face in the puppy's coat and feeling dreadfully sick. I had to sit down on the floor for a few minutes till my knees stopped shaking and the waves of nausea stopped. Then I took up a candle and looked again—a long deliberate look closer to the skeleton, its dry bones gleamed in the flickering light. How long had it been lying there? Long enough for the clothing and flesh to have crumbled to dust; probably many years then. It was the skeleton of a man, the hands and feet were too big for a woman; some quarryman perhaps. The rock must have fallen and killed him and no one had ever found him . . . no one had come into this horrible place since it happened.

Next I forced myself to kneel beside the skeleton and I set a candle on the floor beside me. I held the puppy captive between my knees, then I looked more closely. Something lay inside the rib cavity. With extreme care so as not to touch the bones, I inserted my hand and lifted out an old-fashioned silver watch on a chain. It appeared undamaged though the silver was badly discoloured, almost black. Curiously I turned it over and found on the back an inscription. I blew on it and rubbed it on my sweater till the surface became clearer, and moving the candle closer I was able to make out the words "Rodger Graham 31/10/1899."

I sank back on to my heels and began to tremble all over as the full shock of my discovery hit me—Rodger Graham—I had found the skeleton of Rodger Graham after all those years!

I looked round the grim underground chamber once again. I stared at the slab of stone poised over the entrance to shut off the world outside—he must have been

struck down and killed before he even had time to close it. I gasped at the grizzly collection scattered about on the table, at the sad little animal skeletons on the shelves, —what had Rodger Graham to do with these things; why had he been in this horrible place?

Then I remembered the ghost with its evil aura that had so terrified me—Rodger's ghost. Those grizzly objects must be his; this place was his den, his workroom where he had carried out his secret rites. No wonder he could not rest; no wonder his unhappy spirit haunted Karasay House!

I got stiffly to my feet and picked Merman up, and I carried the candle back to the table. As I put it down I noticed something I had missed before, lettering in white chalk on the stone. I leaned closer and read, "Millie Carpentier and Rodger Graham." The names were linked together by peculiar hieroglyphics that looked like symbols of some sort. Millie Carpentier, my great-grandmother! What could *she* have had to do with this place? Could she have discovered it, known Rodger for what he was? I was shocked to find her name linked to Rodger's. Had he had some horrible hold over her? I could not believe that they had been friends. There was a lot I did not understand, a lot I would never be able to explain, but some of the loose threads were beginning to tighten, and the family story to make sense.

I supposed there would have to be some kind of inquiry when I told of my discovery, and this might bring sensational publicity to the Graham family. At least I could spare Gran the unpleasantness of having her mother's name associated with what I had found; no one need ever know about *her*.

I spat on my hankie and when it was damp enough I used it to rub all the lettering off the table. I took one last look round, then thankfully I turned to go. I sent Merman ahead of me through the tunnel, shooing him along —he couldn't get out fast enough, nor could I. It was marvellous to breathe again the fresh sweet air outside, to feel the salty wind on my face, to hear the pure bird song, to see the clear beauty of the September evening.

I picked Merman up and hurried along the path towards the house. I only looked round once, but when I did I thought I saw Miss Minnie disappearing behind the trees, and I wondered how long she had been there watching me. It might only have been a trick of the light so I did not go back—I was not sure—and in any case I was deadly tired and longing to be home.

CHAPTER FIFTEEN

I MADE FOR THE KITCHEN FIRST, HOPING TO SCROUNGE A late cup of tea, but when I reached the door I heard raised voices. Greenie and Polly seemed to be having a row. In any case Greenie would be busy cooking dinner and not in a suitable frame of mind to listen to my story. So I opened the door just enough to push the puppy inside, and they never even noticed me. They sounded angry with one another though I could not make out what the heated argument was about. It surprised me, Greenie and Polly were usually the best of friends. I'd never heard them quarrelling before. Well, I'd tell Gran and Cousin Derwent my story first.

I went along to the drawing room, but it was empty, so I turned to Cousin Derwent's little study. The door was shut but I tapped on it and went in. He was sitting at his desk, papers and letters spread out before him, a pen in his hand, and he looked thoroughly disgruntled and fed up. Obviously he did not want to be bothered by me or anyone else—perhaps his war wound was hurting and making him tetchy.

"Sorry," I said, "I don't want to interrupt you, but where is Gran?"

"Lying down in her room," he replied, barely looking up. "She had a bit of a headache."

"Oh. Thanks," I said, retreating rapidly.

Whatever was wrong with everyone? Something was at work in the house setting everyone at sixes and sevens, disrupting and disturbing their usual peace. I began to feel angry and frustrated myself, although I was so tired. Here was I with a most peculiar story to tell, and no one willing to hear it! Very well then, I'd just keep it to myself; in fact it might be better to tell no one till the next morning.

I was still feeling pretty shaken over what I had found, so I decided to have a long hot bath to calm me down. When I was relaxed and soothed and ready for dinner I went along to Gran's room and knocked softly on the door. I found her doing her hair and almost ready to go downstairs, her headache nearly gone.

"And what sort of a day did you have, darling?" she asked. "I hope you didn't go too far, you look tired, washed out in fact."

And no wonder! I thought. If you only *knew*.

"I had a gorgeous walk right across the island," I said aloud, "and now I'm ravenous." Gran took my arm and we went downstairs together. As the evening went on, I grew tense and restless; my secret became a burden and I felt weighed down by guilt, as if by finding Rodger's skeleton I had committed a crime. Yet all I had done was to *find* it.

There was no music that night. For the first time since I arrived, Gran and Cousin Derwent seemed edgy with one another and Gran made her headache the excuse for going to bed early. After I had said goodnight to her and Cousin Derwent had gone back into his study, I thought I'd go out for a breath of air before it got too dark. I carried Merman with me for company. His paw was not too bad but I didn't let him walk.

There was the crispness of autumn in the air with just a hint of frost and the sky was thick with stars as I wandered down the road toward Tallows. The windows were lit but I did not go in. I drew comfort and reassurance from knowing that the Autumn People were still there, but somehow I could not disturb their calm with my problem that evening. Something, I did not know what, held me away from the place I most wanted to be.

I twisted the stone ring on my finger and found it was still impossible to take it off; its magic was not yet completed. Then as I realized that it was getting cold and I was wearing only a thin cardigan over my dress, I turned toward home and bed.

As I entered the house I got the same impression that I

had earlier, but now it was much stronger—something was going on, the atmosphere was tense, a storm was brewing, it was as if unseen forces had been raised and were pitted against one another. I felt that I was in the very centre of it, for it was I who had found Rodger.

I should have asked Gran to let me sleep in her room, but my curiosity got the better of me so I stayed in my own. I was very tired, exhausted in fact, so I fell asleep immediately.

The clock in the hall was striking three when I woke. It was pitch dark and quite silent, but the atmosphere in the room was electric: a conflict was going on, with vibrations so strong that a clash of swords would not have surprised me. Waves of intense cold ebbed and flowed as the tension mounted, my ears hummed, and I lay very still in the darkness, my body tense, scarcely daring to breathe. I could see nothing, hear nothing, but I felt shaken, battered, by the nightmarish struggle going on around me.

At last I could stand it no longer. I sprang out of bed and ran along the corridor to Gran's room.

"Can I come in with you, Gran, for a while?" I begged. "I'm having a kind of nightmare and I'm cold."

Gran moved over in the double bed to make room for me and held out her arms. I crept in beside her, and comforted by her slim warmth, soon fell into an exhausted sleep.

When I woke it was daylight, to my surprise a serene and beautiful morning. I lay for a while thinking, trying to decide when to tell people about the skeleton, even whether to tell anyone at all. I shrank from the telling; it was too fine a day to spoil. I decided to wait at least till the evening. I slipped out of bed without disturbing Gran and went into my own room to get dressed. When I reached the kitchen, I found that peace was restored. Greenie and Polly were friends again, laughing happily together. The evil of the night before was gone, perhaps it was losing its power, maybe the night before had exhausted its strength. Or maybe the strange atmosphere had been all in my mind. I didn't know what to think.

Cousin Derwent suddenly surprised us by walking in at the back door. He seemed to be in the best of tempers.

"I thought we might go across to Bransay," he suggested, naming one of the smaller islands. "It's such a glorious day. Would you like that Romilly?"

"I'd love it," I cried gaily. "Can we take Donald's boat?"

"I'll see to it at once," said Cousin Derwent. "Will you pack some sandwiches for us, Greenie, and Polly, let us have some breakfast as soon as you can."

We were away by nine o'clock, dancing over the blue water in Donald's boat. I was out to enjoy myself and I deliberately put all unpleasant thoughts behind me; there would be time enough for all that later on.

It took us nearly two hours to get there, and then there was a walk across from the harbour to the best bay, so that it was time for lunch when we finally got settled. Seals came close to watch us while we ate our sandwiches, their inquisitive heads bobbing up and down in the shallow water; mothers called to their young ones and played with them while the old bulls rolled and blew and grunted close by; and terns dived into the little waves for fish. It was peaceful and lovely and uncomplicated. When we had eaten Gran took out her paperback and settled herself more comfortably to read; and Cousin Derwent got out his sketching pad and crayons, and I too pulled my sketch book and pencil from my pocket and tried to draw—but it was no use, I could not concentrate and nothing came right. My patterns were all vague and distorted. After a while I gave up and wandered off down the beach thinking I might have a swim or scrabble in the rock pools for a bit.

But as soon as I was alone, my problem reared up at me and I had to think about it again—to tell or not to tell about Rodger. My first loyalty was to Gran, and if her mother was in any way involved with him it would be better to keep silence, but how was I to know? Instinctively I thought of Sarah; what would she do in my place? Sarah never vacillated—she made up her mind instantly and plunged right in. I had not much doubt that in my place she'd have gone at once straight to Cousin Derwent and told him the whole story, but would she have been right? Should something so long forgotten be brought to light again? New investigations might do more harm than good and I didn't want Gran or the Graham family hurt. The more I thought about it the more I wanted to hold back and say nothing. When it was time to leave and make our way back to the harbour and Donald's boat, I had come to no decision.

A stiff breeze had sprung up and the crossing was

choppy on the way back. I felt quite chilly in spite of my anorak.

When we landed on Karasay, instead of joining Gran and Cousin Derwent in the car, I decided to walk back up the hill to get warm again.

I started off at a brisk pace, but by the time I came to Miss Juniper's cottage I had to slow down a bit. The windows were closely curtained, the front door shut, and although a feather of smoke blew away from the chimney, there appeared to be no one at home. I wondered where Miss Minnie was and whether her sister was out at one of her mysterious meetings again.

Tallows as I passed it was shuttered and empty, but I promised myself a visit there later in the evening.

When I reached the drive up to Karasay House a sudden whim made me take the path through the copse, the back way into the garden, past the scene of my gruesome discovery. I had no intention whatever of going into the loathsome place ever again. But as I reached the edge of the trees I noticed a strong smell of burning. I stood and sniffed—it was coming from the direction of the cave. I started to run and when I reached the entrance I found a choking cloud of smoke billowing from it—the cave was on fire!

CHAPTER SIXTEEN

I HESITATED FOR ONLY A MOMENT BEFORE I PLUNGED IN. Much as I dreaded it I knew I had to go. Someone must have lighted the fire; someone might be trapped inside the place. I knelt at the entrance and felt in my pocket to make sure the matches were still there, then I whipped off the silk scarf I had worn as a headband all day and tied it over my nose and mouth, and keeping my head close to the ground I crawled into the tunnel. The smoke made my eyes smart till tears ran down my cheeks, and as I went farther in I could see the glow of fire ahead of me. Then just inside the rock chamber I saw a bundle slumped on the floor and I struck a match. It was Miss

Minnie, and she was unconscious. I took a quick look round the cave as the fire in the centre flared up again, and I saw that the whole place had been cleared—Rodger's skeleton, the fox mask, the little animals, the clay figures all were gone, everything had been burnt on the fire, everything—then I turned to Miss Minnie; I had to get her out and quickly.

The next few minutes were the hardest I can ever remember. I wriggled backwards as fast as I could, pulling Miss Minnie through the tunnel. I grew more and more exhausted and breathing became more difficult as I struggled to get her out into the fresh air. She was a good deal heavier than I expected, but at last with a final spurt of effort I managed to pull her clear. I tore the scarf from my face and took some deep gulps of fresh air. Then I rolled Miss Minnie on to her front and blessing my first aid classes at school, I began to give her artificial respiration. At first nothing happened and I began to panic wondering if I ought to leave her and try to get help, but I didn't dare stop, and luckily very soon she started to come round and her colour began to come back. Then she smiled at me.

"Don't try to move," I said, patting her hand. "You must stay here and rest while I go and get help from the house." But she would not hear of it.

"Just give me a minute to get my breath back and I'll be right as rain," she said. "What happened? The last thing I remember is trying to get out of that horrible cave. Where did you find me?"

I told her how I had seen the smoke and gone in after

her and dragged her out. "What were you *doing* in there?" I asked. "How did you find the place and why did you set it on fire, Miss Minnie? You might have died of suffocation in there if I hadn't happened to come along when I did."

"Yes, well . . . I watched you coming out of the cave with the puppy the other evening." So it *had* been Miss Minnie I'd seen after all. "And when you'd gone I went in myself to have a look—a horrible place, an evil place, a den of witchcraft. I could smell it; I've met it before you see. Did you know that Karasay used to be called "The Isle of Witches" and witchcraft is still practiced here? This cave must be one of its sources. It had to be stamped out, destroyed once and for all, every bit of it, and fire is the most powerful purifier. I spent the day gathering dry bracken for kindling and piling it up inside the cave, then I threw everything on top—*everything*—and set it alight, but I wasn't quite quick enough getting myself out. Well, it's done now; it's all over, finished, there's nothing left there to harm anyone."

I had listened to her with mixed feelings. It sounded like the haverings of a crazy old woman, yet I knew that she was partly right; I had seen the place myself, I had felt its evil spell and I was thankful, oh so thankful, that there was nothing left of it.

"I'll go home now," said Miss Minnie, struggling to get onto her feet. I brushed the dust off her dress and helped her up. "I'm proud of this day's work," she remarked with satisfaction.

"Are you sure you're all right?" I asked. "Won't you

come up to the house and let Greenie give you a cup of tea before you go home?"

But she shook her head. She had made up her mind, so I did not try to dissuade her although she was still pale with shock. I took her arm and went with her.

When we reached her cottage I didn't feel at all happy about leaving her.

"Are you *sure* you are all right? Shouldn't you see the doctor?" I asked anxiously.

She smiled at me. "No fuss," she whispered. "We'll keep all this to ourselves. I'll be quite all right now; look —there's my sister peeping from the window."

I put my arms round her and kissed her. "Thank you for what you did," I said. "It was very brave of you."

I walked slowly back up the hill, filled with an enormous feeling of relief. Miss Minnie had solved the problem of the rock chamber for me; now no one need ever know anything about it.

When I reached my room, I crossed to the window and stood looking out over the garden and I felt at peace. Idly I twisted the ring on my finger; unthinking I slid it to the knuckle—*and it slipped right off as easily as it had gone on in the first place.*

I sat down on my bed and stared at it. It took several minutes for me to take in what had happened; then I put the ring carefully into my purse till I made up my mind what to do with it.

I decided to wash my hair and have a bath and to put on my best dress as a kind of celebration. When I was ready I stood on the landing at the top of the stairs, listening, my antennae fully stretched. The house was quiet, serene, and completely . . . ordinary, the tension was gone, the old struggle ended.

Greenie also must have felt in a celebrating mood for she gave us the best dinner I've ever tasted, which Polly served with a beaming smile.

After dinner I left Gran and Cousin Derwent to their music and strolled down the road toward Tallows though I guessed what I would find. The windows were darkened, the house was shuttered and deserted, the Autumn People were gone! Though I had had an inner sense of what to expect I felt suddenly desolate.

I hated to lose them, those Victorian shadows who meant so much to me. I thought of them each in turn, especially of Millie Carpentier and Jocelyn Parsons—I was more than half in love with him myself. What had gone wrong between them, what had broken their romance, ended their love affair? Rodger Graham was at the root of the trouble I felt certain; in some way he had used his power to separate them, to force them apart so that they never came together again.

How Millie must have hated him, and feared him too for the harm he could do. Perhaps she knew of his secret room and what went on there; perhaps when he disappeared she had guessed where he might be and had deliberately kept silent. Was this her secret? Was this why she had never returned to Karasay? Had a nagging sense of guilt kept her away? No one would ever know the truth about what had happened, and perhaps that was best. I stood looking at the house wondering about things I would never know, then I turned and walked slowly home.

Greenie was waiting for me at the side door of the house when I got back.

She put an arm round my shoulders and drew me into the kitchen. Polly had gone out for a while.

She made me sit down by the fire and took both my cold hands in hers as if she understood my dejection and wanted to comfort me.

"They've gone, have they?" she said. "But not for

good, they'll be back again and so will you."

"Oh Greenie," I cried despairingly, "how do you know they haven't stopped coming for ever?"

"They won't leave the house for good before another Romilly takes it over—that's what Catha always said."

"Another Romilly?" I repeated, puzzled. "There isn't another Romilly—only *me!*" I'm the other Romilly! Whatever did she mean? "Tallows can never be mine—how could it be?"

"That remains to be seen, doesn't it?" said Greenie enigmatically.

I slept late next morning and when I woke I felt a deep peace inside though then I remembered that the Autumn People were gone. And yet to me it seemed they were not gone, for even if they never returned, I would always remember them and have their blessing and—what was it Greenie said they wanted to preserve?—their pattern of family tradition, bound up in me. It was a comfort, though I still felt something was missing somewhere.

When eventually I got down for breakfast Gran and Cousin Derwent had finished theirs so I had mine in the kitchen.

"Miss Juniper had a stroke last night, the postman tells me," said Greenie.

"Miss Juniper, not Miss Minnie?" I asked anxiously.

"Miss Juniper, the older sister," Greenie repeated. "Now it's Miss Minnie's turn to be boss."

I couldn't help feeling pleased although I hoped Miss Juniper wasn't too bad, just enough to give Miss Minnie the upper hand for a change. It was a kind of reward for her. Now she'd be able to wear her bright blue stockings whenever she liked!

September was almost over and my holiday was coming to its end, the summer gone. Soon there would be early flurries of snow, the peat fires would be stacked up, curtains would be drawn against the cold and the dark as the island prepared to face the winter.

There was only time for one more expedition and I was allowed to choose. "To the main island, to the museum in Portness where we went before," I begged.

Gran was in a gay mood and Cousin Derwent in the highest spirits, like two children being given a treat, and I couldn't think why, for the day was sunless, the holiday over, and Gran and I about to go south to London leaving Cousin Derwent alone once more.

We battled our way across the bay against a wind that blew from the north, greying the water and whipping it into foam. The little town had changed since last we had been there. Most of the visitors had gone and the shops had emptied, their tourist trade over for the year.

"Alison and I have a little business to see to," Cousin Derwent told me. "Can you look after yourself for an hour or so before lunch?"

"Of course," I said. It gave me the very chance I needed to do what I had come for. I made my way straight to the museum that I had visited once before. There was a collection of stone relics I remembered and wanted to find again. A family of Americans hovered over the cases of primitive implements, exclaiming at the

great age of the exhibits, peering at the photos of the ancient fortresses and the graves of the Viking settlers.

I came to the showcase I had been looking for, a collection of treasures found in a prehistoric grave—arrowheads, beads, ornaments, domestic implements, and two
or three finger rings, all of stone. I waited there till the
Americans caught up with me. The custodian followed
them to explain and inform.

"Gee, boy! Look at those arrowheads!" cried one of
the boys. "Hey, mister, could I hold one in my hand, and
look at it by the window?"

The custodian was just as obliging as I remembered
him; he unlocked the case and took several arrowheads
over to the daylight while the family clustered round
him. It gave me a wonderful chance to carry out the plan
I had made.

Quickly I took the stone ring out of my purse and laid
it carefully beside the others. When the case was re-
locked, no one noticed the extra ring. I breathed a great
sigh of relief; the ring was safely under lock and key, its
magic rendered harmless, its potency in safekeeping.

I spent a few more minutes wandering round, then
strolled back to the hotel on the quay, where I was to
meet Gran and Cousin Derwent for lunch. The fishing
boats had come in and I stopped to watch the catch being
unloaded by the men in their yellow oilskins. When I
turned to go into the hotel, Gran was standing at the window looking on to the quay, and beckoned to me.

She was alone, but she looked very happy. I went to sit
beside her and she slipped her arm through mine.

"I've something to tell you, darling," she said. "Cousin Derwent and I are going to be married. Look—we've just bought the ring."

"Oh Gran, I'm so happy for you both," I cried, hugging her. I wasn't greatly surprised, and it seemed a splendid arrangement for two lonely people.

"Will you live up here on Karasay?" I asked.

"In the summer, yes, but the winter we'll spend in Edinburgh," she said.

"Oh Gran, I'll miss you!" I cried, suddenly nostalgic. "I can't imagine London without you, and Karasay is a very long way from Pembrokeshire."

"We won't lose touch," Gran promised. "I'm much too interested in you and your future to let you forget me."

"As if I ever would!" I cried.

"Now, before Cousin Derwent comes I want to *talk* to you about your future. You know what you want to do, don't you?"

"Oh yes," I replied without hesitation, for everything seemed suddenly to have dropped into place with my morning peace and calm and was splendidly clear to me. "I'm going in for design and that means going to art school to learn about it," I said. "I want to design for all kinds of things—for fabrics, tiles, china, wallpapers—and my designs will be based on natural things, like William Morris's, like my own old flower patterns, distinctive and entirely my own, so that people will recognize them at once as a Romilly Williams design."

Gran was delighted. "You will do very well, I know.

Now, I'd like to help you to go to art school, darling, help you financially I mean. Where do you want to go?"

"I haven't really thought yet," I confessed. "London I suppose, although I don't much want to live there; it's much more Sarah's scene than mine."

"What about Edinburgh?" Gran suggested. "You could live with us to start with till you found your feet, and we'd love to have you, *both* of us would."

"Oh Gran, what a lovely idea!" I exclaimed. Edinburgh had never occurred to me; it might be just the right place for me, a place where one could combine the old and the new to make one's own pattern of life without feeling out of things.

"I'll talk to my parents when I get home," I promised; then jokingly I added, "Of course there *are* little things like exams to be considered before I can even get an entrance! Thank you for thinking of it, Gran; it's a marvellous offer."

When Cousin Derwent arrived, he treated us to a super lunch, and we were a gay party when we stepped into the boat to cross the bay again.

After dinner that evening, I left Gran and Cousin Derwent at the piano and carried the old photograph album to a far corner of the room—I wanted to think.

I turned the pages of photos of the early Grahams till I came to my favourites, the ones of Millie at Karasay, and of the Parsons, my beloved Autumn People. They had given me much happiness and I thought of the hours I had spent, somehow in another time, in their home at Tallows. I thought especially of Jocelyn—Jocelyn who should have been my great-grandfather if things had not gone wrong between him and Millie. Perhaps someday I would be lucky enough to meet a man I could love as Millie had loved Jocelyn and marry him—but not too soon; there were things I wanted to do first.

Grahams and Parsons of a time that was gone, old fogeys perhaps to many of my contemporaries, but to me people with a way of life that had an appeal I did not mean to forget. Roots in the past, a recurring pattern of family life gave me a feeling of strength, a secure sense of continuity, for the essential human experiences were the same in their day as in ours; only the trimmings were different. It was up to me to use from their old pattern what I needed for my own. I knew that my life would be richer because I had known the Autumn People.

EXIT

It was my first term at art school. I was having a wonderful time and the work was fascinating. I had lost some of my shyness and had made some good friends, boys as well as girls, but I had met no one I wanted as a boy friend. Life was exciting and intensely busy. I felt I had come a long way from that September on Karasay, but the Autumn People lingered on in my mind with a haunting sweetness.

Now the term was almost over and I was going home to Pembrokeshire for Christmas. Exams had just finished and I had sent in my piece of work for my report—a pattern of mares-tails, their feathery fronds and dark ringed stems dipping and swaying to the sea wind in a strange primeval ballet. It was to me a symbol of Pembrokeshire and I hoped it might win a prize. On the last Friday of the term a traditional fancy-dress ball was held to which all my friends were going. I had decided to go as my great-grandmother, and with Gran's help we concocted a dress to suit the part, and I practiced wearing my hair up in the correct style.

It was a bitter night with snow in the air and the first flakes were beginning to fall when the carload arrived to pick me up. The hall was quite full when we got there, the noise and excitement overwhelming, and dancing had already begun. When we joined the jostling throng on the floor there was scarcely room to move.

After the first few dances one of my partners, a pirate, led me up onto the balcony to get my breath and went to find us something to drink, and I had a chance to look around over the heads of the crowd.

It was then that I saw him on the other side of the hall, a tall fair young man whose face was very familiar . . . whose face . . . my heart started to hammer in an alarming way and there was a rushing sound in my ears so that I feared I was going to faint. I took a deep breath, blinked my eyes and looked again . . . *it was the face of Jocelyn Parsons.*

For a moment I thought he was a ghost for he looked just the same as when I had seen him at Tallows, and then I remembered that the party was a fancy-dress one. I was still rooted to the spot when after some time my partner returned with our drinks—I drank mine in one gulp.

"What a scrum! Sorry to be so long," he shouted in my ear. "Look, let's try to get across the hall, there's a chap I've been talking to at the bar that you ought to meet; his people are friendly with mine and with yours—Joss Parsons, he's just arrived from Australia. Come on, follow me."

I followed him as if in a dream. Somehow we edged our way round the room to where Jocelyn was standing, and in a moment introductions were being shouted and then my pirate left me, and Joss, in the dress of his great-grandfather, put his hand under my elbow.

"Let's get out of here," he shouted, and he urged me toward the supper room. At least it was quieter there and we sat down at a table together and took a good look at one another.

"What did he say your name is?" he asked.

"Romilly W-Williams," I stuttered. "I know your grandmother, Mrs. Parsons; she is a friend of my grandmother's. I saw her only last week. But what are you doing here? She never said you were coming."

"She didn't know. My father and I flew over yesterday as a surprise for her seventieth birthday—well, partly that, and partly to get me fixed up to read architecture in Edinburgh next year."

"But what are you doing at this party?" I asked.

"Someone fell out at the last minute and I was invited to take his place," Joss explained. "It was a fancy-dress ball and these were the only things handy at the last moment. I found them in the attic."

I felt I was still gawking at him. I couldn't quite believe that he was real, but I wasn't in the least shy of him, only wonderfully, gloriously happy. I was not even truly surprised. I had always known that patterns had to be complete.

"My grandmother is one of the Grahams of Karasay," I told him. "It is strange to meet you here tonight, although we'd have been bound to meet soon anyway since our grandmothers are friends."

"*Now* I know who you are, of course. I've often heard of the Grahams of Karasay. Our families have been friends for years and years haven't they? I'm going to fetch us some food and then we can go on talking," said Joss.

It was a blissful evening. We talked and we danced and we talked again, and all the time as we got to know one another, I imagined the Autumn People bending close to listen and to give us their blessing. I was sure that Millie watched us with special delight, for we were the two, Joss and I, who could complete what she and Jocelyn had begun.

It was late when he took me back to Gran's and we parted on the doorstep.

"See you tomorrow?" he whispered. I felt as if he had set a crown of stars upon my head.

"Tomorrow," I promised, although it was already today.